This Book Belongs to

The Wonderful Oz Books by L. Frank Baum
Published by Ballantine Books

THE TIN WOODMAN OF OZ

A Faithful Story of the Astonishing Adventure
Undertaken by the Tin Woodman, assisted
by Woot the Wanderer, the Scarecrow
of Oz, and Polychrome, the Rainbow's
Daughter

BY

L. FRANK BAUM

"Royal Historian of Oz"

ILLUSTRATED BY

JOHN R. NEILL

A Del Rey Book

BALLANTINE BOOKS · NEW YORK

A Del Rey Book
Published by Ballantine Books

"The Marvelous Land of Oz" Map copyright © 1979 by
James E. Haff and Dick Martin. Reproduced by permission of
The International Wizard of Oz Club, Inc.

Published in the United States by Ballantine Books, a division
of Random House, Inc., New York, and simultaneously in
Canada by Random House of Canada Limited, Toronto.

Library of Congress Catalog Card Number: 80-81570

ISBN 0-345-33436-1

This edition published by arrangement with Contemporary
Books, Inc.

Manufactured in the United States of America

First Ballantine Books Edition: January 1981
Third Printing: October 1985

Cover art by Michael Herring

This Book
is dedicated
to the son of
my son
Frank Alden Baum

Ozma

To My Readers

I know that some of you have been waiting for this story of the Tin Woodman, because many of my correspondents have asked me, time and again, what ever became of the "pretty Munchkin girl" whom Nick Chopper was engaged to marry before the Wicked Witch enchanted his axe and he traded his flesh for tin. I, too, have wondered what became of her, but until Woot the Wanderer interested himself in the matter the Tin Woodman knew no more than we did. However, he found her, after many thrilling adventures, as you will discover when you have read this story.

I am delighted at the continued interest of both young and old in the Oz stories. A learned college professor recently wrote me to ask: "For readers of what age are your books intended?" It puzzled me to answer that properly, until I had looked over some of the letters I have received. One says: "I'm a little boy 5 years old, and I just love your Oz stories. My sister, who is writing this for me, reads me the

Oz books, but I wish I could read them myself." Another letter says: "I'm a great girl 13 years old, so you'll be surprised when I tell you I am not too old yet for the Oz stories." Here's another letter: "Since I was a young girl I've never missed getting a Baum book for Christmas. I'm married, now, but am as eager to get and read the Oz stories as ever." And still another writes: "My good wife and I, both more than 70 years of age, believe that we find more real enjoyment in your Oz books than in any other books we read." Considering these statements, I wrote the college professor that my books are intended for all those whose hearts are young, no matter what their ages may be.

I think I am justified in promising that there will be some astonishing revelations about The Magic of Oz in my book for 1919.

Always your loving and grateful friend,

L. FRANK BAUM.
Royal Historian of Oz.

"OZCOT"
at HOLLYWOOD
in CALIFORNIA
1918.

LIST OF CHAPTERS

PRINCESS
DOROTHY

THE TINWOODMAN OFOZ

Woot

in court dress

Woot the Wanderer

CHAPTER 1

THE Tin Woodman sat on
his glittering tin throne in the
handsome tin hall of his
splendid tin castle in the
Winkie Country of the Land
of Oz. Beside him, in a chair
of woven straw, sat his best
friend, the Scarecrow of Oz.
At times they spoke to one another of curious things they
had seen and strange adventures they had known
since first they two had met and become comrades. But at times they were silent, for these
things had been talked over many times between
them, and they found themselves contented in
merely being together, speaking now and then a
brief sentence to prove they were wide awake

and attentive. But then, these two quaint persons never slept. Why should they sleep, when they never tired?

And now, as the brilliant sun sank low over the Winkie Country of Oz, tinting the glistening tin towers and tin minarets of the tin castle with glorious sunset hues, there approached along a winding pathway Woot the Wanderer, who met at the castle entrance a Winkie servant.

The servants of the Tin Woodman all wore tin helmets and tin breastplates and uniforms covered with tiny tin discs sewed closely together on silver cloth, so that their bodies sparkled as beautifully as did the tin castle—and almost as beautifully as did the Tin Woodman himself.

Woot the Wanderer looked at the man servant—all bright and glittering—and at the magnificent castle—all bright and glittering—and as he looked his eyes grew big with wonder. For Woot was not very big and not very old and, wanderer though he was, this proved the most gorgeous sight that had ever met his boyish gaze.

"Who lives here?" he asked.

"The Emperor of the Winkies, who is the famous Tin Woodman of Oz," replied the servant, who had been trained to treat all strangers with courtesy.

"A Tin Woodman? How queer!" exclaimed the little wanderer.

"Well, perhaps our Emperor *is* queer," admitted the servant; "but he is a kind master and as honest and true as good tin can make him; so we, who gladly serve him, are apt to forget that he is not like other people."

"May I see him?" asked Woot the Wanderer, after a moment's thought.

"If it please you to wait a moment, I will go and ask him," said the servant, and then he went into the hall where the Tin Woodman sat with his friend the Scarecrow. Both were glad to learn that a stranger had arrived at the castle, for this would give them something new to talk about, so the servant was asked to admit the boy at once.

By the time Woot the Wanderer had passed through the grand corridors—all lined with ornamental tin—and under stately tin archways and through the many tin rooms all set with beautiful tin furniture, his eyes had grown bigger than ever and his whole little body thrilled with amazement. But, astonished though he was, he was able to make a polite bow before the throne and to say in a respectful voice: "I salute your Illustrious Majesty and offer you my humble services."

"Very good!" answered the Tin Woodman in his accustomed cheerful manner. "Tell me who you are, and whence you come."

"I am known as Woot the Wanderer," answered the boy, "and I have come, through

3

many travels and by roundabout ways, from my former home in a far corner of the Gillikin Country of Oz."

"To wander from one's home," remarked the Scarecrow, "is to encounter dangers and hardships, especially if one is made of meat and bone. Had you no friends in that corner of the Gillikin Country? Was it not homelike and comfortable?"

To hear a man stuffed with straw speak, and speak so well, quite startled Woot, and perhaps he stared a bit rudely at the Scarecrow. But after a moment he replied:

"I had home and friends, your Honorable Strawness, but they were so quiet and happy and comfortable that I found them dismally stupid. Nothing in that corner of Oz interested me, but I believed that in other parts of the country I would find strange people and see new sights, and so I set out upon my wandering journey. I have been a wanderer for nearly a full year, and now my wanderings have brought me to this splendid castle."

"I suppose," said the Tin Woodman, "that in this year you have seen so much that you have become very wise."

"No," replied Woot, thoughtfully, "I am not at all wise, I beg to assure your Majesty. The more I wander the less I find that I know, for in the Land of Oz much wisdom and many things may be learned."

"To learn is simple. Don't you ask questions?" inquired the Scarecrow.

"Yes; I ask as many questions as I dare; but some people refuse to answer questions."

"That is not kind of them," declared the Tin Woodman. "If one does not ask for information he seldom receives it; so I, for my part, make it a rule to answer any civil question that is asked me."

"So do I," added the Scarecrow, nodding.

"I am glad to hear this," said the Wanderer, "for it makes me bold to ask for something to eat."

"Bless the boy!" cried the Emperor of the Winkies; "how careless of me not to remember that wanderers are usually hungry. I will have food brought you at once."

Saying this he blew upon a tin whistle that was suspended from his tin neck, and at the summons a servant appeared and bowed low. The Tin Woodman ordered food for the stranger, and in a few minutes the servant brought in a tin tray heaped with a choice array of good things to eat, all neatly displayed on tin dishes that were polished till they shone like mirrors. The tray was set upon a tin table drawn before the throne, and the servant placed a tin chair before the table for the boy to seat himself.

"Eat, friend Wanderer," said the Emperor cordially, "and I trust the feast will be to your liking. I, myself, do not eat, being made in such manner that I require no food to keep me alive. Neither does my friend the Scarecrow. But all my Winkie people eat, being formed of flesh, as you are, and so my tin cupboard is never bare, and strangers are always welcome to whatever it contains."

The boy ate in silence for a time, being really hungry, but after his appetite was somewhat satisfied, he said:

"How happened your Majesty to be made of tin, and still be alive?"

"That," replied the tin man, "is a long story."

"The longer the better," said the boy. "Won't you please tell me the story?"

"If you desire it," promised the Tin Woodman, leaning back in his tin throne and crossing his tin legs. "I haven't related my history in a long while, because everyone here knows it nearly as well as I do. But you, being a stranger, are no doubt curious to learn how I became so beautiful and prosperous, so I will recite for your benefit my strange adventures."

"Thank you," said Woot the Wanderer, still eating.

"I was not always made of tin," began the Emperor, "for in the beginning I was a man of flesh and bone and blood and lived in the Munchkin Country of Oz. There I was, by trade, a woodchopper, and contributed my share to the comfort of the Oz people by chopping up the trees of the forest to make firewood, with which the women would cook their meals while the children warmed themselves about the fires. For my home I had a little hut by the edge of the forest, and my life was one of much content until I fell in love with a beautiful Munchkin girl who lived not far away."

"What was the Munchkin girl's name?" asked Woot.

"Nimmie Amee. This girl, so fair that the sunsets blushed when their rays fell upon her, lived with a powerful witch who wore silver shoes and who had made the poor child her slave. Nimmie Amee was obliged to work from morning till night for the old Witch of the East, scrubbing and sweeping her hut and cooking her meals and washing her dishes. She had to cut firewood, too, until I found her one day in the forest and fell in love with her. After that, I always brought plenty of firewood to Nimmie Amee and we became very friendly. Finally I asked her to marry me, and she agreed to do so, but the Witch happened to overhear our conversation and it made her very angry, for she did not wish her slave to be taken away from her. The Witch commanded me never to come near Nimmie Amee again, but

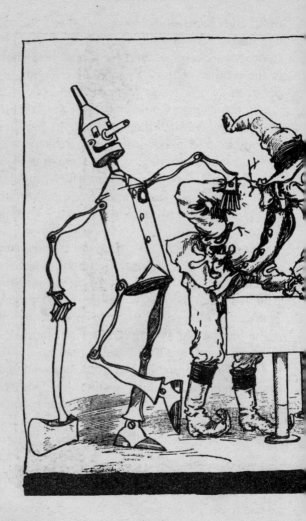

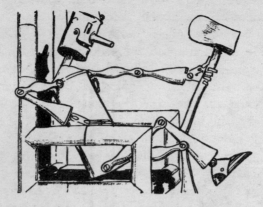

I told her I was my own master and would do as I pleased, not realizing that this was a careless way to speak to a Witch.

"The next day, as I was cutting wood in the forest, the cruel Witch enchanted my axe, so that it slipped and cut off my right leg."

"How dreadful!" cried Woot the Wanderer.

"Yes, it was a seeming misfortune," agreed the Tin Man, "for a one-legged woodchopper is of little use in his trade. But I would not allow the Witch to conquer me so easily. I knew a very skillful mechanic at the other side of the forest, who was my friend, so I hopped on one leg to him and asked him to help me. He soon made me a new leg out of tin and fastened it cleverly to my meat body. It had joints at the knee and at the ankle and was almost as comfortable as the leg I had lost."

"Your friend must have been a wonderful workman!" exclaimed Woot.

"He was, indeed," admitted the Emperor. "He was a tinsmith by trade and could make anything out of tin. When I returned to Nimmie Amee, the girl was delighted and threw her arms around my neck and kissed me, declaring she was proud of me. The Witch saw the kiss and was more angry than before. When I went to work in the forest, next day, my axe, being still enchanted, slipped and cut off my other leg. Again I hopped—on my tin leg—to my friend the tinsmith, who kindly made me another tin leg and fastened it to my body. So I returned joyfully to Nimmie Amee, who was much pleased with my glittering legs and promised that when we were wed she would always keep them oiled and polished. But the Witch was more furious than ever, and as soon as I raised my axe to chop, it twisted around and cut off one of my arms. The tinsmith made me a tin arm and I was not much worried, because Nimmie Amee declared she still loved me."

The Heart of the Tin Woodman

CHAPTER 2

THE Emperor of the Wink-
ies paused in his story to reach
for an oil-can, with which he
carefully oiled the joints in
his tin throat, for his voice
had begun to squeak a little.
Woot the Wanderer, having
satisfied his hunger, watched
this oiling process with much
curiosity, but begged the Tin
Man to go on with his tale.

"The Witch with the Silver Shoes hated me
for having defied her," resumed the Emperor,
his voice now sounding clear as a bell, "and she
insisted that Nimmie Amee should never marry
me. Therefore she made the enchanted axe cut
off my other arm, and the tinsmith also replaced

that member with tin, including these finely-jointed hands that you see me using. But, alas! after that, the axe, still enchanted by the cruel Witch, cut my body in two, so that I fell to the ground. Then the Witch, who was watching from a near-by bush, rushed up and seized the axe and chopped my body into several small pieces, after which, thinking that at last she had destroyed me, she ran away laughing in wicked glee.

"But Nimmie Amee found me. She picked up my arms and legs and head, and made a bundle of them and carried them to the tinsmith, who set to work and made me a fine body of pure tin. When he had joined the arms and legs to the body, and set my head in the tin collar, I was a much better man than ever, for my body could not ache or pain me, and I was so beautiful and bright that I had no need of clothing. Clothing is always a nuisance, because it soils and tears and has to be replaced; but my tin body only needs to be oiled and polished.

"Nimmie Amee still declared she would marry me, as she still loved me in spite of the Witch's evil deeds. The girl declared I would make the brightest husband in all the world, which was quite true. However, the Wicked Witch was not yet defeated. When I returned to my work the axe slipped and cut off my head, which was the only meat part of me then remaining. Moreover,

the old woman grabbed up my severed head and carried it away with her and hid it. But Nimmie Amee came into the forest and found me wandering around helplessly, because I could not see where to go, and she led me to my friend the tinsmith. The faithful fellow at once set to work to make me a tin head, and he had just completed it when Nimmie Amee came running up with my old head, which she had stolen from the Witch. But, on reflection, I considered the tin head far superior to the meat one—I am wearing it yet, so you can see its beauty and grace of outline—and the girl agreed with me that a man all made of tin was far more perfect than one formed of different materials. The tinsmith was as proud of his workmanship as I was, and for three whole days, all admired me and praised my beauty.

"Being now completely formed of tin, I had no more fear of the Wicked Witch, for she was powerless to injure me. Nimmie Amee said we must be married at once, for then she could come to my cottage and live with me and keep me bright and sparkling.

" 'I am sure, my dear Nick,' said the brave and beautiful girl—my name was then Nick Chopper, you should be told—'that you will make the best husband any girl could have. I shall not be obliged to cook for you, for now you do not eat; I shall not have to make your bed, for tin does not tire or require sleep; when we go to a dance, you will not get weary before the music stops and say you want to go home. All day long, while you are chopping wood in the forest, I shall be able to amuse myself in my own way—a privilege few wives enjoy. There is no temper in your new head, so you will not get angry with me. Finally, I shall take pride in being the wife of the only live Tin Woodman in all the world!' Which shows that Nimmie Amee was as wise as she was brave and beautiful."

"I think she was a very nice girl," said Woot the Wanderer. "But, tell me, please, why were you not killed when you were chopped to pieces?"

"In the Land of Oz," replied the Emperor, "no one can ever be killed. A man with a wooden leg or a tin leg is still the same man; and, as I lost parts of my meat body by degrees, I always remained the same person as in the beginning, even though in the end I was all tin and no meat."

"I see," said the boy, thoughtfully. "And did you marry Nimmie Amee?"

"No," answered the Tin Woodman, "I did not. She said she still loved me, but I found that I no longer loved her. My tin body contained no heart, and without a heart no one can love. So the Wicked Witch conquered in the end, and when I left the Munchkin Country of Oz, the poor girl was still the slave of the Witch and had to do her bidding day and night."

"Where did you go?" asked Woot.

"Well, I first started out to find a heart, so I could love Nimmie Amee again; but hearts are more scarce than one would think. One day, in a big forest that was strange to me, my joints suddenly became rusted, because I had forgotten to oil them. There I stood, unable to move hand or foot. And there I continued to stand—while days came and went—until Dorothy and the Scarecrow came along and rescued me. They oiled my joints and set me free, and I've taken good care never to rust again."

"Who was this Dorothy?" questioned the Wanderer.

"A little girl who happened to be in a house when it was carried by a cyclone all the way from Kansas to the Land of Oz. When the house fell, in the Munchkin Country, it fortunately landed on the Wicked Witch and smashed her flat. It was a big house, and I think the Witch is under it yet."

"No," said the Scarecrow, correcting him, "Dorothy says the Witch turned to dust, and the wind scattered the dust in every direction."

"Well," continued the Tin Woodman, "after meeting the Scarecrow and Dorothy, I went with them to the Emerald City, where the Wizard of Oz gave me a heart. But the Wizard's stock of hearts was low, and he gave me a Kind Heart instead of a Loving Heart, so that I could not love Nimmie Amee any more than I did when I was heartless."

"Couldn't the Wizard give you a heart that was both Kind and Loving?" asked the boy.

"No; that was what I asked for, but he said he was so short on hearts, just then, that there was but one in stock, and I could take that or none at all. So I accepted it, and I must say that for its kind it is a very good heart indeed."

"It seems to me," said Woot, musingly, "that the Wizard fooled you. It can't be a very Kind Heart, you know."

"Why not?" demanded the Emperor.

"Because it was unkind of you to desert the girl who loved you, and who had been faithful and true to you when you were in trouble. Had the heart the Wizard gave you been a Kind Heart, you would have gone back home and made the beautiful Munchkin girl your wife, and then brought her here to be an Empress and live in your splendid tin castle."

The Tin Woodman was so surprised at this frank speech that for a time he did nothing but stare hard at the boy Wanderer. But the Scarecrow wagged his stuffed head and said in a positive tone:

"This boy is right. I've often wondered, myself, why you didn't go back and find that poor Munchkin girl."

Then the Tin Woodman stared hard at his friend the Scarecrow. But finally he said in a serious tone of voice:

"I must admit that never before have I thought of such a thing as finding Nimmie Amee and making her Empress of the Winkies. But it is surely not too late, even now, to do this, for the girl must still be living in the Munchkin Country. And, since this strange Wanderer has reminded me of Nimmie Amee, I believe it is my duty to set out and find her. Surely it is not the girl's fault that I no longer love her, and so, if I can make her happy, it is proper that I should do so, and in this way reward her for her faithfulness."

"Quite right, my friend!" agreed the Scarecrow.

"Will you accompany me on this errand?" asked the Tin Emperor.

"Of course," said the Scarecrow.

"And will you take me along?" pleaded Woot the Wanderer in an eager voice.

"To be sure," said the Tin Woodman, "if you care to join our party. It was you who first told me it was my duty to find and marry Nimmie Amee, and I'd like you to know that Nick Chopper, the Tin Emperor of the Winkies, is a man who never shirks his duty, once it is pointed out to him."

"It ought to be a pleasure, as well as a duty, if the girl is so beautiful," said Woot, well pleased with the idea of the adventure.

"Beautiful things may be admired, if not loved," asserted the Tin Man. "Flowers are beautiful, for instance, but we are not inclined to marry them. Duty, on the contrary, is a bugle call to action, whether you are inclined to act, or not. In this case, I obey the bugle call of duty."

"When shall we start?" inquired the Scarecrow, who was always glad to embark upon a new adventure. "I don't hear any bugle, but when do we go?"

"As soon as we can get ready," answered the Emperor. "I'll call my servants at once and order them to make preparations for our journey."

CHAPTER 3

WOOT the Wanderer slept that night in the tin castle of the Emperor of the Winkies and found his tin bed quite comfortable. Early the next morning he rose and took a walk through the gardens, where there were tin fountains and beds of curious tin flowers, and where tin birds perched upon the branches of tin trees and sang songs that sounded like the notes of tin whistles. All these wonders had been made by the clever Winkie tinsmiths, who wound the birds up every morning so that they would move about and sing.

After breakfast the boy went into the throne

21

room, where the Emperor was having his tin joints carefully oiled by a servant, while other servants were stuffing sweet, fresh straw into the body of the Scarecrow.

Woot watched this operation with much interest, for the Scarecrow's body was only a suit of clothes filled with straw. The coat was buttoned tight to keep the packed straw from falling out and a rope was tied around the waist to hold it in shape and prevent the straw from sagging down. The Scarecrow's head was a gunnysack filled with bran, on which the eyes, nose and mouth had been painted. His hands were white cotton gloves stuffed with fine straw. Woot noticed that even when carefully stuffed and patted into shape, the straw man was awkward in his movements and decidedly wobbly on his feet, so the boy wondered if the Scarecrow would be able to travel with them all the way to the forests of the Munchkin Country of Oz.

The preparations made for this important journey were very simple. A knapsack was filled with food and given Woot the Wanderer to carry upon his back, for the food was for his use alone. The Tin Woodman shouldered an axe which was sharp and brightly polished, and the Scarecrow put the Emperor's oil-can in his pocket, that he might oil his friend's joints should they need it.

"Who will govern the Winkie County during

I don't hear
any bugle

your absence?" asked the boy.

"Why, the Country will run itself," answered
the Emperor. "As a matter of fact, my people do
not need an Emperor, for Ozma of Oz watches
over the welfare of all her subjects, including the
Winkies. Like a good many kings and emperors,
I have a grand title, but very little real power,
which allows me time to amuse myself in my
own way. The people of Oz have but one law to
obey, which is: 'Behave Yourself,' so it is easy for
them to abide by this Law, and you'll notice they
behave very well. But it is time for us to be off,
and I am eager to start because I suppose that
that poor Munchkin girl is anxiously awaiting
my coming."

"She's waited a long time already, seems to
me," remarked the Scarecrow, as they left the
grounds of the castle and followed a path that
led eastward.

"True," replied the Tin Woodman; "but I've noticed that the last end of a wait, however long it has been, is the hardest to endure; so I must try to make Nimmie Amee happy as soon as possible."

"Ah; that proves you have a Kind Heart," remarked the Scarecrow, approvingly.

"It's too bad he hasn't a Loving Heart," said Woot. "This Tin Man is going to marry a nice girl through kindness, and not because he loves her, and somehow that doesn't seem quite right."

"Even so, I am not sure it isn't best for the girl," said the Scarecrow, who seemed very intelligent for a straw man, "for a loving husband is not always kind, while a kind husband is sure to make any girl content."

"Nimmie Amee will become an Empress!" announced the Tin Woodman, proudly. "I shall have a tin gown made for her, with tin ruffles and tucks on it, and she shall have tin slippers, and tin earrings and bracelets, and wear a tin crown on her head. I am sure that will delight Nimmie Amee, for all girls are fond of finery."

"Are we going to the Munchkin Country by way of the Emerald City?" inquired the Scarecrow, who looked upon the Tin Woodman as the leader of the party.

"I think not," was the reply. "We are engaged upon a rather delicate adventure, for we are seeking a girl who fears her former lover has forgotten her. It will be rather hard for me, you must admit, when I confess to Nimmie Amee that I have come to marry her because it is my duty to do so, and therefore the fewer witnesses there are to our meeting the better for both of us. After I have found Nimmie Amee and she has managed to control her joy at our reunion, I shall take her to the Emerald City and introduce her to Ozma and Dorothy, and to Betsy Bobbin and Tiny Trot, and all our other friends; but, if I remember rightly, poor Nimmie Amee has a sharp tongue when angry, and she may be a trifle angry with me, at first, because I have been so long in coming to her."

"I can understand that," said Woot gravely. "But how can we get to that part of the Munchkin Country where you once lived without passing through the Emerald City?"

"Why, that is easy," the Tin Man assured him.

"I have a map of Oz in my pocket," persisted the boy, "and it shows that the Winkie Country, where we now are, is at the west of Oz, and the Munchkin Country at the east, while directly between them lies the Emerald City."

"True enough; but we shall go toward the north, first of all, into the Gillikin Country, and so pass around the Emerald City," explained the Tin Woodman.

"That may prove a dangerous journey," re-

plied the boy. "I used to live in one of the top corners of the Gillikin Country, near to Ooga-boo, and I have been told that in this northland country are many people whom it is not pleasant to meet. I was very careful to avoid them during my journey south."

"A Wanderer should have no fear," observed the Scarecrow, who was wobbling along in a funny, haphazard manner, but keeping pace with his friends.

"Fear does not make one a coward," returned Woot, growing a little red in the face, "but I believe it is more easy to avoid danger than to overcome it. The safest way is the best way, even for one who is brave and determined."

"Do not worry, for we shall not go far to the north," said the Emperor. "My one idea is to avoid the Emerald City without going out of our way more than is necessary. Once around the

Emerald City we will turn south into the Munchkin Country, where the Scarecrow and I are well acquainted and have many friends."

"I have traveled some in the Gillikin Country," remarked the Scarecrow, "and while I must say I have met some strange people there at times, I have never yet been harmed by them."

"Well, it's all the same to me," said Woot, with assumed carelessness. "Dangers, when they cannot be avoided, are often quite interesting, and I am willing to go wherever you two venture to go."

So they left the path they had been following and began to travel toward the northeast, and all that day they were in the pleasant Winkie Country, and all the people they met saluted the Emperor with great respect and wished him good luck on his journey. At night they stopped at a house where they were well entertained and where Woot was given a comfortable bed to sleep in.

"Were the Scarecrow and I alone," said the Tin Woodman, "we would travel by night as well as by day; but with a meat person in our party, we must halt at night to permit him to rest."

"Meat tires, after a day's travel," added the Scarecrow, "while straw and tin never tire at all. Which proves," said he, "that we are somewhat superior to people made in the common way."

Woot could not deny that he was tired, and he slept soundly until morning, when he was given a good breakfast, smoking hot.

"You two miss a great deal by not eating," he said to his companions.

"It is true," responded the Scarecrow. "We miss suffering from hunger, when food cannot be had, and we miss a stomach-ache, now and then."

As he said this, the Scarecrow glanced at the Tin Woodman, who nodded his assent.

All that second day they traveled steadily, entertaining one another the while with stories of adventures they had formerly met and listening to the Scarecrow recite poetry. He had learned a great many poems from Professor Wogglebug and loved to repeat them whenever any-body would listen to him. Of course Woot and the Tin Woodman now listened, because they could not do otherwise—unless they rudely ran away from their stuffed comrade.

One of the Scarecrow's recitations was like this:

"What sound is so sweet
    As the straw from the wheat
When it crunkles so tender and low?
    It is yellow and bright,
    So it gives me delight
To crunkle wherever I go.

"Sweet, fresh, golden Straw!
    There is surely no flaw
In a stuffing so clean and compact.
    It creaks when I walk,
    And it thrills when I talk,
And its fragrance is fine, for a fact.

"To cut me don't hurt,
    For I've no blood to squirt,
And I therefore can suffer no pain;
    The straw that I use
    Doesn't lump up or bruise,
Though it's pounded again and again!

"I know it is said
    That my beautiful head
Has brains of mixed wheat-straw and bran,

But my thoughts are so good
I'd not change, if I could,
For the brains of a common meat man.

"Content with my lot,
I'm glad that I'm not
Like others I meet day by day;
If my insides get musty,
Or mussed-up, or dusty,
I get newly stuffed right away."

CHAPTER 4

TOWARD evening, the travelers found there was no longer a path to guide them, and the purple hues of the grass and trees warned them that they were now in the Country of the Gillikins, where strange peoples dwelt in places that were quite unknown to the other inhabitants of Oz. The fields were wild and uncultivated and there were no houses of any sort to be seen. But our friends kept on walking even after the sun went down, hoping to find a good place for Woot the Wanderer to sleep; but when it grew quite dark and the boy was weary with his long walk, they halted right in the middle of a field and allowed Woot to get his supper from the food he carried in his knapsack. Then the Scarecrow laid himself down, so that Woot could use his stuffed body as a pillow, and the Tin Woodman stood up beside them all night, so the dampness of the ground might not rust his joints or dull his brilliant polish. Whenever the dew settled on his body he carefully wiped it off with a cloth, and so in the morning the Emperor shone as brightly as ever in the rays of the rising sun.

They wakened the boy at daybreak, the Scarecrow saying to him:

"We have discovered something queer, and therefore we must counsel together what to do about it."

"What have you discovered?" asked Woot, rubbing the sleep from his eyes with his knuckles and giving three wide yawns to prove he was fully awake.

"A Sign," said the Tin Woodman. "A Sign, and another path."

"What does the Sign say?" inquired the boy.

"It says that 'All Strangers are Warned not to Follow this Path to Loonville,'" answered the Scarecrow, who could read very well when his eyes had been freshly painted.

"In that case," said the boy, opening his knapsack to get some breakfast, "let us travel in some other direction."

But this did not seem to please either of his companions.

"I'd like to see what Loonville looks like," remarked the Tin Woodman.

"When one travels, it is foolish to miss any interesting sight," added the Scarecrow.

"But a warning means danger," protested Woot the Wanderer, "and I believe it sensible to keep out of danger whenever we can."

They made no reply to this speech for a while. Then said the Scarecrow:

"I have escaped so many dangers, during my lifetime, that I am not much afraid of anything that can happen."

"Nor am I!" exclaimed the Tin Woodman, swinging his glittering axe around his tin head, in a series of circles. "Few things can injure tin, and my axe is a powerful weapon to use against a foe. But our boy friend," he continued, looking

33

solemnly at Woot, "might perhaps be injured if the people of Loonville are really dangerous; so I propose he waits here while you and I, Friend Scarecrow, visit the forbidden City of Loonville."

"Don't worry about me," advised Woot, calmly. "Wherever you wish to go, I will go, and share your dangers. During my wanderings I have found it more wise to keep out of danger than to venture in, but at that time I was alone, and now I have two powerful friends to protect me."

So, when he had finished his breakfast, they all set out along the path that led to Loonville.

"It is a place I have never heard of before," remarked the Scarecrow, as they approached a dense forest. "The inhabitants may be people, of some sort, or they may be animals, but whatever they prove to be, we will have an interesting story to relate to Dorothy and Ozma on our return."

The path led into the forest, but the big trees grew so closely together and the vines and underbrush were so thick and matted that they had to clear a path at each step in order to proceed. In one or two places the Tin Man, who went first to clear the way, cut the branches with a blow of his axe. Woot followed next, and last of the three came the Scarecrow, who could not have kept the path at all had not his comrades broken the way for his straw-stuffed body.

Presently the Tin Woodman pushed his way through some heavy underbrush, and almost tumbled headlong into a vast cleared space in the forest. The clearing was circular, big and roomy, yet the top branches of the tall trees reached over and formed a complete dome or roof for it. Strangely enough, it was not dark in this immense natural chamber in the woodland, for the place glowed with a soft, white light that seemed to come from some unseen source.

In the chamber were grouped dozens of queer creatures, and these so astonished the Tin Man that Woot had to push his metal body aside, that he might see, too. And the Scarecrow pushed Woot aside, so that the three travelers stood in a row, staring with all their eyes.

The creatures they beheld were round and ball-like; round in body, round in legs and arms, round in hands and feet and round of head. The only exception to the roundness was a slight hollow on the top of each head, making it saucer-shaped instead of dome-shaped. They wore no clothes on their puffy bodies, nor had they any hair. Their skins were all of a light gray color, and their eyes were mere purple spots. Their noses were as puffy as the rest of them.

"Are they rubber, do you think?" asked the Scarecrow, who noticed that the creatures bounded, as they moved, and seemed almost as light as air.

"It is difficult to tell what they are," answered Woot, "they seem to be covered with warts."

The Loons—for so these folks were called—had been doing many things, some playing together, some working at tasks and some gathered in groups to talk; but at the sound of strange voices, which echoed rather loudly through the clearing, all turned in the direction of the intruders. Then, in a body, they all rushed forward, running and bounding with tremendous speed.

The Tin Woodman was so surprised by this sudden dash that he had no time to raise his axe before the Loons were on them. The creatures swung their puffy hands, which looked like boxing-gloves, and pounded the three travelers as hard as they could, on all sides. The blows were quite soft and did not hurt our friends at all, but the onslaught quite bewildered them, so that in a brief period all three were knocked over and fell flat upon the ground. Once down, many of the Loons held them, to prevent their getting up again, while others wound long tendrils of vines about them, binding their arms and legs to their bodies and so rendering them helpless.

"Aha!" cried the biggest Loon of all; "we've got 'em safe; so let's carry 'em to King Bal and have 'em tried, and condemned and perforated!"

They had to drag their captives to the center of the domed chamber, for their weight, as com-

pared with that of the Loons, prevented their
being carried. Even the Scarecrow was much
heavier than the puffy Loons. But finally the
party halted before a raised platform, on which
stood a sort of throne, consisting of a big, wide
chair with a string tied to one arm of it. This
string led upward to the roof of the dome.

Arranged before the platform, the prisoners
were allowed to sit up, facing the empty throne.

"Good!" said the big Loon who had commanded the party. "Now to get King Bal to judge
these terrible creatures we have so bravely captured."

As he spoke he took hold of the string and
began to pull as hard as he could. One or two of
the others helped him and pretty soon, as they
drew in the cord, the leaves above them parted
and a Loon appeared at the other end of the
string. It didn't take long to draw him down to
the throne, where he seated himself and was
tied in, so he wouldn't float upward again.

"Hello," said the King, blinking his purple
eyes at his followers; "what's up now?"

"Strangers, your Majesty—strangers and captives," replied the big Loon, pompously.

"Dear me! I see 'em. I see 'em very plainly,"
exclaimed the King, his purple eyes bulging out
as he looked at the three prisoners. "What curious animals! Are they dangerous, do you think,
my good Panta?"

"I'm 'fraid so, your Majesty. Of course, they may *not* be dangerous, but we mustn't take chances. Enough accidents happen to us poor Loons as it is, and my advice is to condemn and perforate 'em as quickly as possible."

"Keep your advice to yourself," said the monarch, in a peeved tone. "Who's King here, anyhow? You or Me?"

"We made you our King because you have less common sense than the rest of us," answered Panta Loon, indignantly. "I could have been King myself, had I wanted to, but I didn't care for the hard work and responsibility."

As he said this, the big Loon strutted back and forth in the space between the throne of King Bal and the prisoners, and the other Loons seemed much impressed by his defiance. But suddenly there came a sharp report and Panta Loon instantly disappeared, to the great astonishment of the Scarecrow, the Tin Woodman and Woot the Wanderer, who saw on the spot where the big fellow had stood a little heap of flabby, wrinkled skin that looked like a collapsed rubber balloon.

"There!" exclaimed the King; "I expected that would happen. The conceited rascal wanted to puff himself up until he was bigger than the rest of you, and this is the result of his folly. Get the pump working, some of you, and blow him up again."

"We will have to mend the puncture first, your Majesty," suggested one of the Loons, and the prisoners noticed that none of them seemed surprised or shocked at the sad accident to Panta.

"All right," grumbled the King. "Fetch Til to mend him."

One or two ran away and presently returned, followed by a lady Loon wearing huge, puffed-up rubber skirts. Also she had a purple feather fastened to a wart on the top of her head, and around her waist was a sash of fibre-like vines, dried and tough, that looked like strings.

"Get to work, Til," commanded King Bal. "Panta has just exploded."

The lady Loon picked up the bunch of skin and examined it carefully until she discovered a hole in one foot. Then she pulled a strand of string from her sash, and drawing the edges of the hole together, she tied them fast with the string, thus making one of those curious warts which the strangers had noticed on so many Loons. Having done this, Til Loon tossed the bit of skin to the other Loons and was about to go away when she noticed the prisoners and stopped to inspect them.

"Dear me!" said Til; "what dreadful creatures. Where did they come from?"

"We captured them," replied one of the Loons.

"And what are we going to do with them?" inquired the girl Loon.

"Perhaps we'll condemn 'em and puncture 'em," answered the King.

"Well," said she, still eyeing the captives, "I'm not sure they'll puncture. Let's try it, and see."

One of the Loons ran to the forest's edge and quickly returned with a long, sharp thorn. He glanced at the King, who nodded his head in assent, and then he rushed forward and stuck the thorn into the leg of the Scarecrow. The Scarecrow merely smiled and said nothing, for the thorn didn't hurt him at all.

Then the Loon tried to prick the Tin Woodman's leg, but the tin only blunted the point of the thorn.

"Just as I thought," said Til, blinking her purple eyes and shaking her puffy head; but just then the Loon stuck the thorn into the leg of Woot the Wanderer, and while it had been blunted somewhat, it was still sharp enough to hurt.

"Ouch!" yelled Woot, and kicked out his leg with so much energy that the frail bonds that tied him burst apart. His foot caught the Loon—who was leaning over him—full on his puffy stomach, and sent him shooting up into the air. When he was high over their heads he exploded with a loud "pop" and his skin fell to the ground.

"I really believe," said the King, rolling his

spot-like eyes in a frightened way, "that Panta was right in claiming these prisoners are dangerous. Is the pump ready?"

Some of the Loons had wheeled a big machine in front of the throne and now took Panta's skin and began to pump air into it. Slowly it swelled out until the King cried "Stop!"

"No, no!" yelled Panta, "I'm not big enough yet."

"You're as big as you're going to be," declared the King. "Before you exploded you were bigger than the rest of us, and that caused you to be proud and overbearing. Now you're a little smaller than the rest, and you will last longer and be more humble."

"Pump me up—pump me up!" wailed Panta. "If you don't you'll break my heart."

"If we do we'll break your skin," replied the King.

So the Loons stopped pumping air into Panta, and pushed him away from the pump. He was certainly more humble than before his accident, for he crept into the background and said nothing more.

"Now pump up the other one," ordered the King. Til had already mended him, and the Loons set to work to pump him full of air.

During these last few moments none had paid much attention to the prisoners, so Woot, finding his legs free, crept over to the Tin Wood-

man and rubbed the bonds that were still around his arms and body against the sharp edge of the axe, which quickly cut them.

The boy was now free, and the thorn which the Loon had stuck into his leg was lying unnoticed on the ground, where the creature had dropped it when he exploded. Woot leaned forward and picked up the thorn, and while the Loons were busy watching the pump, the boy sprang to his feet and suddenly rushed upon the group.

"Pop"—"pop"—"pop!" went three of the Loons, when the Wanderer pricked them with his thorn, and at the sounds the others looked around and saw their danger. With yells of fear they bounded away in all directions, scattering about the clearing, with Woot the Wanderer in full chase. While they could run much faster than the boy, they often stumbled and fell, or got in one another's way, so he managed to catch several and prick them with his thorn.

It astonished him to see how easily the Loons exploded. When the air was let out of them they were quite helpless. Til Loon was one of those who ran against his thorn and many others suffered the same fate. The creatures could not escape from the enclosure, but in their fright many bounded upward and caught branches of the trees, and then climbed out of reach of the dreaded thorn.

Woot was getting pretty tired chasing them, so he stopped and came over, panting, to where his friends were sitting, still bound.

"Very well done, my Wanderer," said the Tin Woodman. "It is evident that we need fear these puffed-up creatures no longer, so be kind enough to unfasten our bonds and we will proceed upon our journey."

Woot untied the bonds of the Scarecrow and helped him to his feet. Then he freed the Tin Woodman, who got up without help. Looking around them, they saw that the only Loon now remaining within reach was Bal Loon, the King, who had remained seated in his throne, watching the punishment of his people with a bewildered look in his purple eyes.

"Shall I puncture the King?" the boy asked his companions.

King Bal must have overheard the question for he fumbled with the cord that fastened him to the throne and managed to release it. Then he floated upward until he reached the leafy dome, and parting the branches he disappeared from sight. But the string that was tied to his body was still connected with the arm of the throne, and they knew they could pull his Majesty down again, if they wanted to.

"Let him alone," suggested the Scarecrow. "He seems a good enough king for his peculiar people, and after we are gone, the Loons will have something of a job to pump up all those whom Woot has punctured."

"Every one of them ought to be exploded," declared Woot, who was angry because his leg still hurt him.

"No," said the Tin Woodman, "that would not be just fair. They were quite right to capture us, because we had no business to intrude here, having been warned to keep away from Loonville. This is their country, not ours, and since the poor things can't get out of the clearing, they can harm no one save those who venture here out of curiosity, as we did."

"Well said, my friend," agreed the Scarecrow. "We really had no right to disturb their peace and comfort; so let us go away."

They easily found the place where they had forced their way into the enclosure, so the Tin

Woodman pushed aside the underbrush and started first along the path. The Scarecrow followed next and last came Woot, who looked back and saw that the Loons were still clinging to their perches on the trees and watching their former captives with frightened eyes.

"I guess they're glad to see the last of us," remarked the boy, and laughing at the happy ending of the adventure, he followed his comrades along the path.

Mrs. Yoop, the Giantess

CHAPTER 5

WHEN they had reached the end of the path, where they had first seen the warning sign, they set off across the country in an easterly direction. Before long they reached Rolling Lands, which were a succession of hills and valleys where constant climbs and descents were required, and their journey now became tedious, because on climbing each hill, they found before them nothing in the valley below it—except grass, or weeds or stones.

Up and down they went for hours, with nothing to relieve the monotony of the landscape, until finally, when they had topped a higher hill than usual, they discovered a cup-shaped valley before them in the center of which stood an enormous castle, built of purple stone. The castle was high and broad and long, but had no turrets and towers. So far as they could see, there was but one small window and one big door on each side of the great building.

"This is strange!" mused the Scarecrow. "I'd no idea such a big castle existed in this Gillikin Country. I wonder who lives here?"

"It seems to me, from this distance," remarked the Tin Woodman, "that it's the biggest castle I ever saw. It is really too big for any use, and no one could open or shut those big doors without a stepladder."

"Perhaps, if we go nearer, we shall find out whether anybody lives there or not," suggested Woot. "Looks to me as if nobody lived there."

On they went, and when they reached the center of the valley, where the great stone castle stood, it was beginning to grow dark. So they hesitated as to what to do.

"If friendly people happen to live here," said Woot, "I shall be glad of a bed; but should enemies occupy the place, I prefer to sleep upon the ground."

"And if no one at all lives here," added the Scarecrow, "we can enter, and take possession, and make ourselves at home."

While speaking he went nearer to one of the

great doors, which was three times as high and broad as any he had ever seen in a house before, and then he discovered, engraved in big letters upon a stone over the doorway, the words:

"YOOP CASTLE"

"Oho!" he exclaimed; "I know the place now. This was probably the home of Mr. Yoop, a terrible giant whom I have seen confined in a cage, a long way from here. Therefore this castle is likely to be empty and we may use it in any way we please."

"Yes, yes," said the Tin Emperor, nodding; "I also remember Mr. Yoop. But how are we to get into his deserted castle? The latch of the door is so far above our heads that none of us can reach it."

They considered this problem for a while, and then Woot said to the Tin Man:

"If I stand upon your shoulders, I think I can unlatch the door."

"Climb up, then," was the reply, and when the boy was perched upon the tin shoulders of Nick Chopper, he was just able to reach the latch and raise it.

At once the door swung open, its great hinges making a groaning sound as if in protest, so Woot leaped down and followed his companions into a big, bare hallway. Scarcely were the three inside, however, when they heard the door slam shut behind them, and this astonished them

because no one had touched it. It had closed of its own accord, as if by magic. Moreover, the latch was on the outside, and the thought occurred to each one of them that they were now prisoners in this unknown castle.

"However," mumbled the Scarecrow, "we are not to blame for what cannot be helped; so let us push bravely ahead and see what may be seen."

It was quite dark in the hallway, now that the outside door was shut, so as they stumbled along a stone passage they kept close together, not knowing what danger was likely to befall them.

Suddenly a soft glow enveloped them. It grew brighter, until they could see their surroundings distinctly. They had reached the end of the passage and before them was another huge door. This noiselessly swung open before them, without the help of anyone, and through the doorway they observed a big chamber, the walls of which were lined with plates of pure gold, highly polished.

This room was also lighted, although they could discover no lamps, and in the center of it was a great table at which sat an immense woman. She was clad in silver robes embroidered with gay floral designs, and wore over this splendid raiment a short apron of elaborate lace-work. Such an apron was no protection, and was not in keeping with the handsome gown, but the huge woman wore it, nevertheless. The table at which she sat was spread with a white cloth and had golden dishes upon it, so the travelers saw that they had surprised the Giantess while she was eating her supper.

She had her back toward them and did not even turn around, but taking a biscuit from a dish she began to butter it and said in a voice that was big and deep but not especially unpleasant:

"Why don't you come in and allow the door to shut? You're causing a draught, and I shall catch cold and sneeze. When I sneeze, I get cross, and when I get cross I'm liable to do something wicked. Come in, you foolish strangers; come in!"

Being thus urged, they entered the room and approached the table, until they stood where they faced the great Giantess. She continued eating, but smiled in a curious way as she looked at them. Woot noticed that the door had closed silently after they had entered, and that didn't please him at all.

"Well," said the Giantess, "what excuse have you to offer?"

"We didn't know anyone lived here, Madam," explained the Scarecrow; "so, being travelers and strangers in these parts, and wishing to find a place for our boy friend to sleep, we ventured to enter your castle."

"You knew it was private property, I suppose?" said she, buttering another biscuit.

"We saw the words, 'Yoop Castle,' over the door, but we knew that Mr. Yoop is a prisoner in a cage in a far-off part of the land of Oz, so we decided there was no one now at home and that we might use the castle for the night."

"I see," remarked the Giantess, nodding her head and smiling again in that curious way—a way that made Woot shudder. "You didn't know that Mr. Yoop was married, or that after he was cruelly captured his wife still lived in his castle and ran it to suit herself."

"Who captured Mr. Yoop?" asked Woot, looking gravely at the big woman.

"Wicked enemies. People who selfishly objected to Yoop's taking their cows and sheep for his food. I must admit, however, that Yoop had a bad temper, and had the habit of knocking over a few houses, now and then, when he was angry. So one day the little folks came in a great crowd and captured Mr. Yoop, and carried him away to a cage somewhere in the mountains. I don't know where it is, and I don't care, for my husband treated me badly at times, forgetting the respect a giant owes to a giantess. Often he kicked me on my shins, when I wouldn't wait on him. So I'm glad he is gone."

"It's a wonder the people didn't capture you, too," remarked Woot.

"Well, I was too clever for them," said she, giving a sudden laugh that caused such a breeze that the wobbly Scarecrow was almost blown off his feet and had to grab his friend Nick Chopper to steady himself. "I saw the people coming," continued Mrs. Yoop, "and knowing they meant mischief I transformed myself into a mouse and hid in a cupboard. After they had gone away, carrying my shin-kicking husband with them, I transformed myself back to my former shape again, and here I've lived in peace and comfort ever since."

"Are you a Witch, then?" inquired Woot.

"Well, not exactly a Witch," she replied, "but I'm an Artist in Transformations. In other words, I'm more of a Yookoohoo than a Witch, and of course you know that the Yookoohoos are the cleverest magic-workers in the world."

The travelers were silent for a time, uneasily considering this statement and the effect it might have on their future. No doubt the Giantess had wilfully made them her prisoners; yet she spoke so cheerfully, in her big voice, that until now they had not been alarmed in the least.

By and by the Scarecrow, whose mixed brains had been working steadily, asked the woman:

"Are we to consider you our friend, Mrs. Yoop, or do you intend to be our enemy?"

"I never have friends," she said in a matter-of-fact tone, "because friends get too familiar and

56

always forget to mind their own business. But I am not your enemy; not yet, anyhow. Indeed, I'm glad you've come, for my life here is rather lonely. I've had no one to talk to since I transformed Polychrome, the Daughter of the Rainbow, into a canary-bird."

"How did you manage to do that?" asked the Tin Woodman, in amazement. "Polychrome is a powerful fairy!"

"She *was*," said the Giantess; "but now she's a canary-bird. One day after a rain, Polychrome danced off the Rainbow and fell asleep on a little mound in this valley, not far from my castle. The sun came out and drove the Rainbow away, and before Poly wakened, I stole out and transformed her into a canary-bird in a gold cage studded with diamonds. The cage was so she couldn't fly away. I expected she'd sing and talk and we'd have good times together; but she has proved no company for me at all. Ever since the moment of her transformation, she has refused to speak a single word."

"Where is she now?" inquired Woot, who had heard tales of lovely Polychrome and was much interested in her.

"The cage is hanging up in my bedroom," said the Giantess, eating another biscuit.

The travelers were now more uneasy and suspicious of the Giantess than before. If Polychrome, the Rainbow's Daughter, who was a

real fairy, had been transformed and enslaved by this huge woman, who claimed to be a Yookoohoo, what was liable to happen to *them*? Said the Scarecrow, twisting his stuffed head around in Mrs. Yoop's direction:

"Do you know, Ma'am, who we are?"

"Of course," said she; "a straw man, a tin man and a boy."

"We are very important people," declared the Tin Woodman.

"All the better," she replied. "I shall enjoy your society the more on that account. For I mean to keep you here as long as I live, to amuse me when I get lonely. And," she added slowly, "in this Valley no one ever dies."

They didn't like this speech at all, so the Scarecrow frowned in a way that made Mrs. Yoop smile, while the Tin Woodman looked so fierce that Mrs. Yoop laughed. The Scarecrow suspected she was going to laugh, so he slipped behind his friends to escape the wind from her breath. From this safe position he said warningly:

"We have powerful friends who will soon come to rescue us."

"Let them come," she returned, with an accent of scorn. "When they get here they will find neither a boy, nor a tin man, nor a scarecrow, for tomorrow morning I intend to transform you all into other shapes, so that you cannot be recognized."

This threat filled them with dismay. The good-natured Giantess was more terrible than they had imagined. She could smile and wear pretty clothes and at the same time be even more cruel than her wicked husband had been.

Both the Scarecrow and the Tin Woodman tried to think of some way to escape from the castle before morning, but she seemed to read their thoughts and shook her head.

"Don't worry your poor brains," said she. "You can't escape me, however hard you try. But why should you wish to escape? I shall give you new forms that are much better than the ones you now have. Be contented with your fate, for discontent leads to unhappiness, and unhappiness, in any form, is the greatest evil that can befall you."

"What forms do you intend to give us?" asked Woot earnestly.

"I haven't decided, as yet. I'll dream over it tonight, so in the morning I shall have made up my mind how to transform you. Perhaps you'd prefer to choose your own transformations?"

"No," said Woot, "I prefer to remain as I am."

"That's funny," she retorted. "You are little, and you're weak; as you are, you're not much account, anyhow. The best thing about you is

that you're alive, for I shall be able to make of you some sort of live creature which will be a great improvement on your present form."

She took another biscuit from a plate and dipped it in a pot of honey and calmly began eating it.

The Scarecrow watched her thoughtfully.

"There are no fields of grain in your Valley," said he; "where, then, did you get the flour to make your biscuits?"

"Mercy me! do you think I'd bother to make biscuits out of flour?" she replied. "That is altogether too tedious a process for a Yookoohoo. I set some traps this afternoon and caught a lot of field-mice, but as I do not like to eat mice, I transformed them into hot biscuits for my supper. The honey in this pot was once a wasp's nest, but since being transformed it has become sweet and delicious. All I need do, when I wish to eat, is to take something I don't care to keep, and transform it into any sort of food I like, and eat it. Are you hungry?"

"I don't eat, thank you," said the Scarecrow.

"Nor do I," said the Tin Woodman.

"I have still a little natural food in my knapsack," said Woot the Wanderer, "and I'd rather eat that than any wasp's nest."

"Every one to his taste," said the Giantess carelessly, and having now finished her supper she rose to her feet, clapped her hands together, and the supper table at once disappeared.

The Magic of a Yookoohoo

CHAPTER 6

WOOT had seen very little of magic during his wanderings, while the Scarecrow and the Tin Woodman had seen a great deal of many sorts in their lives, yet all three were greatly impressed by Mrs. Yoop's powers. She did not affect any mysterious airs or indulge in chants or mystic rites, as most witches do, nor was the Giantess old and ugly or disagreeable in face or manner. Nevertheless, she frightened her prisoners more than any witch could have done.

"Please be seated," she said to them, as she sat herself down in a great arm-chair and spread her beautiful embroidered skirts for them to admire. But all the chairs in the room were so high that our friends could not climb to the seats of them. Mrs. Yoop observed this and waved her hand, when instantly a golden ladder appeared leaning against a chair opposite her own.

"Climb up," said she, and they obeyed, the Tin Man and the boy assisting the more clumsy Scarecrow. When they were all seated in a row on the cushion of the chair, the Giantess continued: "Now tell me how you happened to travel in this direction, and where you came from and what your errand is."

So the Tin Woodman told her all about Nimmie Amee, and how he had decided to find her and marry her, although he had no Loving Heart. The story seemed to amuse the big woman, who then began to ask the Scarecrow questions and for the first time in her life heard of Ozma of Oz, and of Dorothy and Jack Pumpkinhead and Dr. Pipt and Tik-Tok and many other Oz people who are well known in the Emerald City. Also Woot had to tell his story, which was very simple and did not take long. The Giantess laughed heartily when the boy related their adventure at Loonville, but said she knew nothing of the Loons because she never left her Valley.

"There are wicked people who would like to capture me, as they did my giant husband, Mr.

Yoop," said she; "so I stay at home and mind my own business."

"If Ozma knew that you dared to work magic without her consent, she would punish you severely," declared the Scarecrow, "for this castle is in the Land of Oz, and no persons in the Land of Oz are permitted to work magic except Glinda the Good and the little Wizard who lives with Ozma in the Emerald City."

"*That* for your Ozma!" exclaimed the Giantess, snapping her fingers in derision. "What do I care for a girl whom I have never seen and who has never seen me?"

"But Ozma is a fairy," said the Tin Woodman, "and therefore she is very powerful. Also, we are under Ozma's protection, and to injure us in any way would make her extremely angry."

"What I do here, in my own private castle in this secluded Valley—where no one comes but fools like you—can never be known to your fairy Ozma," returned the Giantess. "Do not seek to frighten me from my purpose, and do not allow yourselves to be frightened, for it is best to meet bravely what cannot be avoided. I am now going to bed, and in the morning I will give you all new forms, such as will be more interesting to me than the ones you now wear. Good night, and pleasant dreams."

Saying this, Mrs. Yoop rose from her chair and walked through a doorway into another room. So heavy was the tread of the Giantess that even the walls of the big stone castle trembled as she stepped. She closed the door of her bedroom behind her, and then suddenly the light went out and the three prisoners found themselves in total darkness.

The Tin Woodman and the Scarecrow didn't mind the dark at all, but Woot the Wanderer felt worried to be left in this strange place in this strange manner, without being able to see any danger that might threaten.

"The big woman might have given me a bed, anyhow," he said to his companions, and scarcely had he spoken when he felt something press against his legs, which were then dangling from the seat of the chair. Leaning down, he put out his hand and found that a bedstead had appeared, with mattress, sheets and covers, all complete. He lost no time in slipping down upon the bed and was soon fast asleep.

During the night the Scarecrow and the Emperor talked in low tones together, and they got out of the chair and moved all about the room, feeling for some hidden spring that might open a door or window and permit them to escape.

Morning found them still unsuccessful in the quest and as soon as it was daylight Woot's bed suddenly disappeared, and he dropped to the floor with a thump that quickly wakened him. And after a time the Giantess came from her bedroom, wearing another dress that was quite as elaborate as the one in which she had been attired the evening before, and also wearing the pretty lace apron. Having seated herself in a chair, she said:

"I'm hungry; so I'll have breakfast at once."

She clapped her hands together and instantly the table appeared before her, spread with snowy linen and laden with golden dishes. But there was no food upon the table, nor anything else except a pitcher of water, a bundle of weeds and a handful of pebbles. But the Giantess poured some water into her coffee-pot, patted it once or twice with her hand, and then poured out a cupful of steaming hot coffee.

"Would you like some?" she asked Woot.

He was suspicious of magic coffee, but it smelled so good that he could not resist it; so he answered: "If you please, Madam."

The Giantess poured out another cup and set it on the floor for Woot. It was as big as a tub, and the golden spoon in the saucer beside the cup was so heavy the boy could scarcely lift it. But Woot managed to get a sip of the coffee and found it delicious.

Mrs. Yoop next transformed the weeds into a dish of oatmeal, which she ate with good appetite.

"Now, then," said she, picking up the pebbles, "I'm wondering whether I shall have fish-balls

or lamb-chops to complete my meal. Which would you prefer, Woot the Wanderer?"

"If you please, I'll eat the food in my knapsack," answered the boy. "Your magic food might taste good, but I'm afraid of it."

The woman laughed at his fears and transformed the pebbles into fish-balls.

"I suppose you think that after you had eaten this food it would turn to stones again and make you sick," she remarked; "but that would be impossible. *Nothing I transform ever gets back to its former shape again,* so these fish-balls can never more be pebbles. That is why I have to be careful of my transformations," she added, busily eating while she talked, "for while I can change forms at will I can never change them back again—which proves that even the powers of a clever Yookoohoo are limited. When I have transformed you three people, you must always wear the shapes that I have given you."

"Then please don't transform us," begged Woot, "for we are quite satisfied to remain as we are."

"I am not expecting to satisfy you, but intend to please myself," she declared, "and my pleasure is to give you new shapes. For, if by chance your friends came in search of you, not one of them would be able to recognize you."

Her tone was so positive that they knew it would be useless to protest. The woman was not unpleasant to look at; her face was not cruel; her voice was big but gracious in tone; but her words showed that she possessed a merciless heart and no pleadings would alter her wicked purpose.

Mrs. Yoop took ample time to finish her breakfast and the prisoners had no desire to hurry her, but finally the meal was concluded and she folded her napkin and made the table disappear by clapping her hands together. Then she turned to her captives and said:

"The next thing on the programme is to change your forms."

"Have you decided what forms to give us?" asked the Scarecrow, uneasily.

"Yes; I dreamed it all out while I was asleep. This Tin Man seems a very solemn person"— indeed, the Tin Woodman *was* looking solemn, just then, for he was greatly disturbed—"so I shall change him into an Owl."

All she did was to point one finger at him as she spoke, but immediately the form of the Tin Woodman began to change and in a few seconds Nick Chopper, the Emperor of the Winkies, had been transformed into an Owl, with eyes as big as saucers and a hooked beak and strong claws. But he was still tin. He was a Tin Owl, with tin legs and beak and eyes and feathers. When he flew to the back of a chair and perched upon it, his tin feathers rattled against one another with a tinny clatter.

The Giantess seemed much amused by the Tin Owl's appearance, for her laugh was big and jolly.

"You're not liable to get lost," said she, "for your wings and feathers will make a racket wherever you go. And, on my word, a Tin Owl is so rare and pretty that it is an improvement on the ordinary bird. I did not intend to make you tin, but I forgot to wish you to be meat. However, tin you were, and tin you are, and as it's too late to change you, that settles it."

Until now the Scarecrow had rather doubted the possibility of Mrs. Yoop's being able to transform him, or his friend the Tin Woodman, for they were not made as ordinary people are. He had worried more over what might happen to Woot than to himself, but now he began to worry about himself.

"Madam," he said hastily, "I consider this action very impolite. It may even be called rude, considering we are your guests."

"You are not guests, for I did not invite you here," she replied.

"Perhaps not; but we craved hospitality. We threw ourselves upon your mercy, so to speak, and we now find you have no mercy. Therefore, if you will excuse the expression, I must say it is downright wicked to take our proper forms away from us and give us others that we do not care for."

"Are you trying to make me angry?" she asked, frowning.

"By no means," said the Scarecrow; "I'm just trying to make you act more ladylike."

"Oh, indeed! In *my* opinion, Mr. Scarecrow, you are now acting like a bear—so a Bear you shall be!"

Again the dreadful finger pointed, this time in the Scarecrow's direction, and at once his form

began to change. In a few seconds he had become a small Brown Bear, but he was stuffed with straw as he had been before, and when the little Brown Bear shuffled across the floor he was just as wobbly as the Scarecrow had been and moved just as awkwardly.

Woot was amazed, but he was also thoroughly frightened.

"Did it hurt?" he asked the little Brown Bear.

"No, of course not," growled the Scarecrow in the Bear's form; "but I don't like walking on four legs; it's undignified."

"Consider *my* humiliation!" chirped the Tin Owl, trying to settle its tin feathers smoothly with its tin beak. "And I can't see very well, either. The light seems to hurt my eyes."

"That's because you are an Owl," said Woot. "I think you will see better in the dark."

"Well," remarked the Giantess, "I'm very well pleased with these new forms, for my part, and I'm sure you will like them better when you get used to them. So now," she added, turning to the boy, "it is *your* turn."

"Don't you think you'd better leave me as I am?" asked Woot in a trembling voice.

"No," she replied, "I'm going to make a Monkey of you. I love monkeys—they're so cute!—and I think a Green Monkey will be lots of fun and amuse me when I am sad."

Woot shivered, for again the terrible magic finger pointed, and pointed directly his way. He felt himself changing; not so very much, however, and it didn't hurt him a bit. He looked down at his limbs and body and found that his clothes were gone and his skin covered with a fine, silk-like green fur. His hands and feet were now those of a monkey. He realized he really *was* a monkey, and his first feeling was one of anger. He began to chatter as monkeys do. He bounded to the seat of a giant chair, and then to its back and with a wild leap sprang upon the laughing Giantess. His idea was to seize her hair and pull it out by the roots, and so have revenge for her wicked transformations. But she raised her hand and said:

"Gently, my dear Monkey—gently! You're not angry; you're happy as can be!"

Woot stopped short. No; he wasn't a bit angry now; he felt as good-humored and gay as ever he did when a boy. Instead of pulling Mrs. Yoop's hair, he perched on her shoulder and smoothed her soft cheek with his hairy paw. In return, she smiled at the funny green animal and patted his head.

"Very good," said the Giantess. "Let us all become friends and be happy together. How is my Tin Owl feeling?"

"Quite comfortable," said the Owl. "I don't like it, to be sure, but I'm not going to allow my new form to make me unhappy. But, tell me, please: What is a Tin Owl good for?"

"You are only good to make me laugh," replied the Giantess.

"Will a stuffed Bear also make you laugh?" inquired the Scarecrow, sitting back on his haunches to look up at her.

"Of course," declared the Giantess; "and I have added a little magic to your transformations to make you all contented with wearing your new forms. I'm sorry I didn't think to do that when I transformed Polychrome into a Canary-Bird. But perhaps, when she sees how cheerful you are, she will cease to be silent and sullen and take to singing. I will go get the bird and let you see her."

With this, Mrs. Yoop went into the next room and soon returned bearing a golden cage in

which sat upon a swinging perch a lovely yellow Canary.

"Polychrome," said the Giantess, "permit me to introduce to you a Green Monkey, which used to be a boy called Woot the Wanderer, and a Tin Owl, which used to be a Tin Wood-man named Nick Chopper, and a straw-stuffed little Brown Bear which used to be a live Scare-crow."

"We already know one another," declared the Scarecrow. "The bird is Polychrome, the Rainbow's Daughter, and she and I used to be good friends."

"Are you really my old friend, the Scarecrow?" asked the bird, in a sweet, low voice.

"There!" cried Mrs. Yoop; "that's the first time she has spoken since she was transformed."

"I am really your old friend," answered the Scarecrow; "but you must pardon me for appearing just now in this brutal form."

"I am a bird, as you are, dear Poly," said the Tin Woodman; "but, alas! a Tin Owl is not as beautiful as a Canary-Bird."

"How dreadful it all is!" sighed the Canary. "Couldn't you manage to escape from this terrible Yookoohoo?"

"No," answered the Scarecrow, "we tried to escape, but failed. She first made us her prisoners and then transformed us. But how did she manage to get *you*, Polychrome?"

"I was asleep, and she took unfair advantage of me," answered the bird sadly. "Had I been awake, I could easily have protected myself."

"Tell me," said the Green Monkey earnestly, as he came close to the cage, "what must we do, Daughter of the Rainbow, to escape from these transformations? Can't you help us, being a Fairy?"

"At present I am powerless to help even myself," replied the Canary.

"That's the exact truth!" exclaimed the Giantess, who seemed pleased to hear the bird talk, even though it complained; "you are all helpless and in my power, so you may as well make up your minds to accept your fate and be content. Remember that you are transformed for good, since no magic on earth can break your enchantments. I am now going out for my morning walk, for each day after breakfast I walk sixteen times around my castle for exercise. Amuse yourselves while I am gone, and when I return I hope to find you all reconciled and happy."

So the Giantess walked to the door by which our friends had entered the great hall and spoke one word: "Open!" Then the door swung open and after Mrs. Yoop had passed out it closed again with a snap as its powerful bolts shot into place. The Green Monkey had rushed toward the opening, hoping to escape, but he was too late and only got a bump on his nose as the door slammed shut.

The Lace Apron

CHAPTER 7

"NOW," said the Canary, in a tone more brisk than before, "we may talk together more freely, as Mrs. Yoop cannot hear us. Perhaps we can figure out a way to escape."

"Open!" said Woot the Monkey, still facing the door; but his command had no effect and he slowly rejoined the others.

"You cannot open any door or window in this enchanted castle unless you are wearing the Magic Apron," said the Canary.

"What Magic Apron do you mean?" asked the Tin Owl, in a curious voice.

"The lace one, which the Giantess always

wears. I have been her prisoner, in this cage, for several weeks, and she hangs my cage in her bedroom every night, so that she can keep her eye on me," explained Polychrome the Canary. "Therefore I have discovered that it is the Magic Apron that opens the doors and windows, and nothing else can move them. When she goes to bed, Mrs. Yoop hangs her apron on the bedpost, and one morning she forgot to put it on when she commanded the door to open, and the door would not move. So then she put on the lace apron and the door obeyed her. That was how I learned the magic power of the apron."

"I see—I see!" said the little Brown Bear, wagging his stuffed head. "Then, if we could get the apron from Mrs. Yoop, we could open the doors and escape from our prison."

"That is true, and it is the plan I was about to suggest," replied Polychrome the Canary-Bird. "However, I don't believe the Owl could steal the apron, or even the Bear, but perhaps the Monkey could hide in her room at night and get the apron while she is asleep."

"I'll try it!" cried Woot the Monkey. "I'll try it this very night, if I can manage to steal into her bedroom."

"You mustn't think about it, though," warned the bird, "for she can read your thoughts whenever she cares to do so. And do not forget, before you escape, to take me with you. Once I am out of the power of the Giantess, I may discover a way to save us all."

"We won't forget our fairy friend," promised the boy; "but perhaps you can tell me how to get into the bedroom."

"No," declared Polychrome, "I cannot advise you as to that. You must watch for a chance, and slip in when Mrs. Yoop isn't looking."

They talked it over for a while longer and then Mrs. Yoop returned. When she entered, the door opened suddenly, at her command, and closed as soon as her huge form had passed through the doorway. During that day she entered her bedroom several times, on one errand or another, but always she commanded the door to close behind her and her prisoners found not the slightest chance to leave the big hall in which they were confined.

The Green Monkey thought it would be wise to make a friend of the big woman, so as to gain her confidence, so he sat on the back of her chair and chattered to her while she mended her stockings and sewed silver buttons on some golden shoes that were as big as row-boats. This pleased the Giantess and she would pause at times to pat the Monkey's head. The little Brown Bear curled up in a corner and lay still all day. The Owl and the Canary found they could converse together in the bird language, which neither the Giantess nor the Bear nor the Monkey could understand; so at times they twittered away to each other and passed the long, dreary day quite cheerfully.

After dinner Mrs. Yoop took a big fiddle from a big cupboard and played such loud and dreadful music that her prisoners were all thankful when at last she stopped and said she was going to bed.

After cautioning the Monkey and Bear and Owl to behave themselves during the night, she picked up the cage containing the Canary and, going to the door of her bedroom, commanded it to open. Just then, however, she remembered she had left her fiddle lying upon a table, so she went back for it and put it away in the cupboard, and while her back was turned the Green Monkey slipped through the open door into her bedroom and hid underneath the bed. The Giantess, being sleepy, did not notice this, and entering her room she made the door close behind her and then hung the bird-cage on a peg by the window. Then she began to undress, first taking off the lace apron and laying it over the bedpost, where it was within easy reach of her hand.

As soon as Mrs. Yoop was in bed the lights all went out, and Woot the Monkey crouched under the bed and waited patiently until he heard the Giantess snoring. Then he crept out and in the dark felt around until he got hold of the apron, which he at once tied around his own waist.

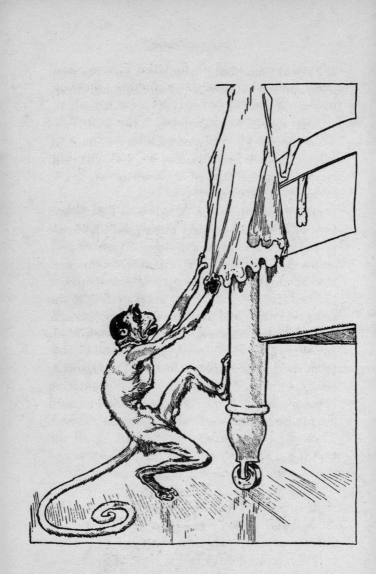

Next, Woot tried to find the Canary, and there was just enough moonlight showing through the window to enable him to see where the cage hung; but it was out of his reach. At first he was tempted to leave Polychrome and escape with his other friends, but remembering his promise to the Rainbow's Daughter Woot tried to think how to save her.

A chair stood near the window, and this—showing dimly in the moonlight—gave him an idea. By pushing against it with all his might, he found he could move the giant chair a few inches at a time. So he pushed and pushed until the chair was beneath the bird-cage, and then he sprang noiselessly upon the seat—for his monkey form enabled him to jump higher than he could do as a boy—and from there to the back of the chair, and so managed to reach the cage and

take it off the peg. Then down he sprang to the floor and made his way to the door.

"Open!" he commanded, and at once the door obeyed and swung open. But his voice wakened Mrs. Yoop, who gave a wild cry and sprang out of bed with one bound. The Green Monkey dashed through the doorway, carrying the cage with him, and before the Giantess could reach the door it slammed shut and imprisoned her in her own bed-chamber!

The noise she made, pounding upon the door, and her yells of anger and dreadful threats of vengeance, filled all our friends with terror, and Woot the Monkey was so excited that in the dark he could not find the outer door of the hall. But the Tin Owl could see very nicely in the dark, so he guided his friends to the right place and when all were grouped before the door Woot commanded it to open. The Magic Apron proved as powerful as when it had been worn by the Giantess, so a moment later they had rushed through the passage and were standing in the fresh night air outside the castle, free to go wherever they willed.

The Menace of the Forest

CHAPTER 8

"QUICK!" cried Polychrome the Canary; "we must hurry, or Mrs. Yoop may find some way to recapture us, even now. Let us get out of her Valley as soon as possible."

So they set off toward the east, moving as swiftly as they could, and for a long time they could hear the yells and struggles of the imprisoned Giantess. The Green Monkey could run over the ground very swiftly, and he carried with him the bird-cage containing Polychrome the Rainbow's Daughter. Also the Tin Owl could skip and fly along at a good rate of speed, his feathers rattling against one another with a tinkling sound as he moved. But the little Brown Bear, being stuffed with straw, was a clumsy traveler and the others had to wait for him to follow.

However, they were not very long in reaching the ridge that led out of Mrs. Yoop's Valley, and when they had passed this ridge and descended into the next valley they stopped to rest, for the Green Monkey was tired.

"I believe we are safe, now," said Polychrome, when her cage was set down and the others had all gathered around it, "for Mrs. Yoop dares not go outside of her own Valley, for fear of being captured by her enemies. So we may take our time to consider what to do next."

"I'm afraid poor Mrs. Yoop will starve to death, if no one lets her out of her bedroom," said Woot, who had a heart as kind as that of the Tin Woodman. "We've taken her Magic Apron away, and now the doors will never open."

"Don't worry about that," advised Polychrome. "Mrs. Yoop has plenty of magic left to console her."

"Are you sure of that?" asked the Green Monkey.

"Yes, for I've been watching her for weeks," said the Canary. "She has six magic hairpins, which she wears in her hair, and a magic ring which she wears on her thumb and which is invisible to all eyes except those of a fairy, and magic bracelets on both her ankles. So I am positive that she will manage to find a way out of her prison."

"She might transform the door into an archway," suggested the little Brown Bear.

"That would be easy for her," said the Tin Owl; "but I'm glad she was too angry to think of that before we got out of her Valley."

"Well, we have escaped the big woman, to be sure," remarked the Green Monkey, "but we still wear the awful forms the cruel yookoohoo gave us. How are we going to get rid of these shapes, and become ourselves again?"

None could answer that question. They sat around the cage, brooding over the problem, until the Monkey fell asleep. Seeing this, the Canary tucked her head under her wing and also slept, and the Tin Owl and the Brown Bear did not disturb them until morning came and it was broad daylight.

"I'm hungry," said Woot, when he wakened, for his knapsack of food had been left behind at the castle.

"Then let us travel on until we can find something for you to eat," returned the Scarecrow Bear.

"There is no use in your lugging my cage any farther," declared the Canary. "Let me out, and throw the cage away. Then I can fly with you and find my own breakfast of seeds. Also I can search for water, and tell you where to find it."

So the Green Monkey unfastened the door of the golden cage and the Canary hopped out. At first she flew high in the air and made great circles overhead, but after a time she returned and perched beside them.

"At the east, in the direction we were following," announced the Canary, "there is a fine forest, with a brook running through it. In the forest there may be fruits or nuts growing, or berry bushes at its edge, so let us go that way."

They agreed to this and promptly set off, this time moving more deliberately. The Tin Owl, which had guided their way during the night, now found the sunshine very trying to his big eyes, so he shut them tight and perched upon the back of the little Brown Bear, which carried the Owl's weight with ease. The Canary sometimes perched upon the Green Monkey's shoulder and sometimes fluttered on ahead of the party, and in this manner they traveled in good spirits across that valley and into the next one to the east of it.

This they found to be an immense hollow, shaped like a saucer, and on its farther edge appeared the forest which Polychrome had seen from the sky.

"Come to think of it," said the Tin Owl, waking up and blinking comically at his friends, "there's no object, now, in our traveling to the Munchkin Country. My idea in going there was to marry Nimmie Amee, but however much the Munchkin girl may have loved a Tin Woodman, I cannot reasonably expect her to marry a Tin Owl."

"There is some truth in that, my friend," remarked the Brown Bear. "And to think that I, who was considered the handsomest Scarecrow in the world, am now condemned to be a scrubby, no-account beast, whose only redeeming feature is that he is stuffed with straw!"

"Consider *my* case, please," said Woot. "The cruel Giantess has made a Monkey of a Boy, and that is the most dreadful deed of all!"

"Your color is rather pretty," said the Brown Bear, eyeing Woot critically. "I have never seen a pea-green monkey before, and it strikes me you are quite gorgeous."

"It isn't so bad to be a bird," asserted the Canary, fluttering from one to another with a free and graceful motion, "but I long to enjoy my own shape again."

"As Polychrome, you were the loveliest maiden I have ever seen—except, of course, Ozma," said the Tin Owl; "so the Giantess did well to transform you into the loveliest of all birds, if you were to be transformed at all. But tell me, since you are a fairy, and have a fairy wisdom: do you think we shall be able to break these enchantments?"

"Queer things happen in the Land of Oz,"

replied the Canary, again perching on the Green Monkey's shoulder and turning one bright eye thoughtfully toward her questioner. "Mrs. Yoop has declared that none of her transformations can ever be changed, even by herself, but I believe that if we could get to Glinda, the Good Sorceress, she might find a way to restore us to our natural shapes. Glinda, as you know, is the most powerful Sorceress in the world, and there are few things she cannot do if she tries."

"In that case," said the Little Brown Bear, "let us return southward and try to get to Glinda's castle. It lies in the Quadling Country, you know, so it is a good way from here."

"First, however, let us visit the forest and search for something to eat," pleaded Woot. So they continued on to the edge of the forest, which consisted of many tall and beautiful trees. They discovered no fruit trees, at first, so the Green Monkey pushed on into the forest depths and the others followed close behind him.

They were traveling quietly along, under the shade of the trees, when suddenly an enormous jaguar leaped upon them from a limb and with one blow of his paw sent the little Brown Bear tumbling over and over until he was stopped by a tree-trunk. Instantly they all took alarm. The Tin Owl shrieked: "Hoot—hoot!" and flew straight up to the branch of a tall tree, although he could scarcely see where he was going. The

Canary swiftly darted to a place beside the Owl, and the Green Monkey sprang up, caught a limb, and soon scrambled to a high perch of safety.

The Jaguar crouched low and with hungry eyes regarded the little Brown Bear, which slowly got upon its feet and asked reproachfully:

"For goodness' sake, Beast, what were you trying to do?"

"Trying to get my breakfast," answered the Jaguar with a snarl, "and I believe I've succeeded. You ought to make a delicious meal—unless you happen to be old and tough."

"I'm worse than that, considered as a breakfast," said the Bear, "for I'm only a skin stuffed with straw, and therefore not fit to eat."

"Indeed!" cried the Jaguar, in a disappointed voice; "then you must be a magic Bear, or enchanted, and I must seek my breakfast from among your companions."

With this he raised his lean head to look up at the Tin Owl and the Canary and the Monkey, and he lashed his tail upon the ground and growled as fiercely as any jaguar could.

"My friends are enchanted, also," said the little Brown Bear.

"All of them?" asked the Jaguar.

"Yes. The Owl is tin, so you couldn't possibly eat him. The Canary is a fairy—Polychrome, the Daughter of the Rainbow—and you never could catch her because she can easily fly out of your reach."

"There still remains the Green Monkey," remarked the Jaguar hungrily. "He is neither made of tin nor stuffed with straw, nor can he fly. I'm pretty good at climbing trees, myself, so I think I'll capture the Monkey and eat him for my breakfast."

Woot the Monkey, hearing this speech from his perch on the tree, became much frightened, for he knew the nature of jaguars and realized they could climb trees and leap from limb to limb with the agility of cats. So he at once began to scamper through the forest as fast as he could go, catching at a branch with his long monkey arms and swinging his green body through space to grasp another branch in a neighboring tree, and so on, while the Jaguar followed him from below, his eyes fixed steadfastly on his prey. But presently Woot got his feet tangled in the Lace Apron, which he was still wearing, and that tripped him in his flight and made him fall to the ground, where the Jaguar placed one huge paw upon him and said grimly:

"I've got you, now!"

The fact that the Apron had tripped him made Woot remember its magic powers, and in his terror he cried out: "Open!" without stopping to consider how this command might save him. But, at the word, the earth opened at the exact spot where he lay under the Jaguar's paw, and his body sank downward, the earth closing over it again. The last thing Woot the Monkey saw, as he glanced upward, was the Jaguar peering into the hole in astonishment.

"He's gone!" cried the beast, with a long-drawn sigh of disappointment; "he's gone, and now I shall have no breakfast."

The clatter of the Tin Owl's wings sounded above him, and the little Brown Bear came trotting up and asked:

"Where is the monkey? Have you eaten him so quickly?"

"No, indeed," answered the Jaguar. "He disappeared into the earth before I could take one bite of him!"

And now the Canary perched upon a stump, a little way from the forest beast, and said:

"I am glad our friend has escaped you; but, as it is natural for a hungry beast to wish his breakfast, I will try to give you one."

"Thank you," replied the Jaguar. "You're rather small for a full meal, but it's kind of you to sacrifice yourself to my appetite."

"Oh, I don't intend to be eaten, I assure you," said the Canary, "but as I am a fairy I know something of magic, and though I am now transformed into a bird's shape, I am sure I can conjure up a breakfast that will satisfy you."

"If you can work magic, why don't you break the enchantment you are under and return to your proper form?" inquired the beast doubtingly.

"I haven't the power to do that," answered the Canary, "for Mrs. Yoop, the Giantess who transformed me, used a peculiar form of yookoohoo magic that is unknown to me. However, she could not deprive me of my own fairy knowledge so I will try to get you a breakfast."

"Do you think a magic breakfast would taste good, or relieve the pangs of hunger I now suffer?" asked the Jaguar.

"I am sure it would. What would you like to eat?"

"Give me a couple of fat rabbits," said the beast.

"Rabbits! No, indeed. I'd not allow you to eat

the dear little things," declared Polychrome the Canary.

"Well, three or four squirrels, then," pleaded the Jaguar.

"Do you think me so cruel?" demanded the Canary, indignantly. "The squirrels are my especial friends."

"How about a plump owl?" asked the beast. "Not a tin one, you know, but a real meat owl."

"Neither beast nor bird shall you have," said Polychrome in a positive voice.

"Give me a fish, then; there's a river a little way off," proposed the Jaguar.

"No living thing shall be sacrificed to feed you," returned the Canary.

"Then what in the world do you expect me to eat?" said the Jaguar in a scornful tone.

"How would mush-and-milk do?" asked the Canary.

The Jaguar snarled in derision and lashed his tail against the ground angrily.

"Give him some scrambled eggs on toast, Poly," suggested the Bear Scarecrow. "He ought to like that."

"I will," responded the Canary, and fluttering her wings she made a flight of three circles around the stump. Then she flew up to a tree and the Bear and the Owl and the Jaguar saw that upon the stump had appeared a great green

leaf upon which was a large portion of scrambled eggs on toast, smoking hot.

"There!" said the Bear; "eat your breakfast, friend Jaguar, and be content."

The Jaguar crept closer to the stump and sniffed the fragrance of the scrambled eggs. They smelled so good that he tasted them, and they tasted so good that he ate the strange meal in a hurry, proving he had been really hungry.

"I prefer rabbits," he muttered, licking his chops, "but I must admit the magic breakfast has filled my stomach full, and brought me comfort. So I'm much obliged for the kindness, little Fairy, and I'll now leave you in peace."

Saying this, he plunged into the thick underbrush and soon disappeared, although they could hear his great body crashing through the bushes until he was far distant.

"That was a good way to get rid of the savage

beast, Poly," said the Tin Woodman to the Canary; "but I'm surprised that you didn't give our friend Woot a magic breakfast, when you knew he was hungry."

"The reason for that," answered Polychrome, "was that my mind was so intent on other things that I quite forgot my power to produce food by magic. But where *is* the monkey boy?"

"Gone!" said the Scarecrow Bear, solemnly. "The earth has swallowed him up."

The Quarrelsome Dragons

CHAPTER 9

THE Green Monkey sank
gently into the earth for a
little way and then tumbled
swiftly through space, land-
ing on a rocky floor with a
thump that astonished him.
Then he sat up, found that no
bones were broken, and gazed
around him.

He seemed to be in a big
underground cave, which was dimly lighted by
dozens of big round discs that looked like moons.
They were not moons, however, as Woot discovered when he had examined the place more
carefully. They were eyes. The eyes were in the
heads of enormous beasts whose bodies trailed far
behind them. Each beast was bigger than an

elephant, and three times as long, and there were a dozen or more of the creatures scattered here and there about the cavern. On their bodies were big scales, as round as pie-plates, which were beautifully tinted in shades of green, purple and orange. On the ends of their long tails were clusters of jewels. Around the great, moon-like eyes were circles of diamonds which sparkled in the subdued light that glowed from the eyes.

Woot saw that the creatures had wide mouths and rows of terrible teeth and, from tales he had heard of such beings, he knew he had fallen into a cavern inhabited by the great Dragons that had been driven from the surface of the earth and were only allowed to come out once in a hundred years to search for food. Of course he had never seen Dragons before, yet there was no mistaking them, for they were unlike any other living creatures.

Woot sat upon the floor where he had fallen, staring around, and the owners of the big eyes returned his look, silently and motionless. Finally one of the Dragons which was farthest away from him asked, in a deep, grave voice:

"What was that?"

And the greatest Dragon of all, who was just in front of the Green Monkey, answered in a still deeper voice:

"It is some foolish animal from Outside."

"Is it good to eat?" inquired a smaller Dragon

beside the great one. "I'm hungry."

"Hungry!" exclaimed all the Dragons, in a reproachful chorus; and then the great one said chidingly: "Tut-tut, my son! You've no reason to be hungry at *this* time."

"Why not?" asked the little Dragon. "I haven't eaten anything in eleven years."

"Eleven years is nothing," remarked another Dragon, sleepily opening and closing his eyes; "I haven't feasted for eighty-seven years, and I dare not get hungry for a dozen or so years to come. Children who eat between meals should be broken of the habit."

"All I had, eleven years ago, was a rhinoceros, and that's not a full meal at all," grumbled the young one. "And, before that, I had waited sixty-two years to be fed; so it's no wonder I'm hungry."

"How old are you now?" asked Woot, forgetting his own dangerous position in his interest in the conversation.

"Why, I'm—I'm— How old am I, Father?" asked the little Dragon.

"Goodness gracious! what a child to ask questions. Do you want to keep me thinking all the time? Don't you know that thinking is very bad for Dragons?" returned the big one, impatiently.

"How old am I, Father?" persisted the small Dragon.

"About six hundred and thirty, I believe. Ask your mother."

"No; don't!" said an old Dragon in the background; "haven't I enough worries, what with being wakened in the middle of a nap, without being obliged to keep track of my children's ages?"

"You've been fast asleep for over sixty years, Mother," said the child Dragon. "How long a nap do you wish?"

"I should have slept forty years longer. And this strange little green beast should be punished for falling into our cavern and disturbing us."

"I didn't know you were here, and I didn't know I was going to fall in," explained Woot.

"Nevertheless, here you are," said the great Dragon, "and you have carelessly wakened our entire tribe; so it stands to reason you must be punished."

"In what way?" inquired the Green Monkey, trembling a little.

"Give me time and I'll think of a way. You're in no hurry, are you?" asked the great Dragon.

"No, indeed," cried Woot. "Take your time. I'd much rather you'd all go to sleep again, and punish me when you wake up in a hundred years or so."

"Let me eat him!" pleaded the littlest Dragon.

"He is too small," said the father. "To eat this one Green Monkey would only serve to make you hungry for more, and there *are* no more."

"Quit this chatter and let me get to sleep," protested another Dragon, yawning in a fearful manner, for when he opened his mouth a sheet of flame leaped forth from it and made Woot jump back to get out of its way.

In his jump he bumped against the nose of a Dragon behind him, which opened its mouth to growl and shot another sheet of flame at him. The flame was bright, but not very hot, yet Woot screamed with terror and sprang forward with a great bound. This time he landed on the paw of the great Chief Dragon, who angrily raised his other front paw and struck the Green Monkey a fierce blow. Woot went sailing through the air and fell sprawling upon the rocky floor far beyond the place where the Dragon Tribe was grouped.

All the great beasts were now thoroughly wakened and aroused, and they blamed the monkey for disturbing their quiet. The littlest Dragon darted after Woot and the others turned their unwieldy bodies in his direction and followed, flashing from their eyes and mouths flames which lighted up the entire cavern.

Woot almost gave himself up for lost, at that moment, but he scrambled to his feet and dashed away to the farthest end of the cave, the Dragons

following more leisurely because they were too clumsy to move fast. Perhaps they thought there was no need of haste, as the monkey could not escape from the cave. But, away up at the end of the place, the cavern floor was heaped with tumbled rocks, so Woot, with an agility born of fear, climbed from rock to rock until he found himself crouched against the cavern roof. There he waited, for he could go no farther, while on over the tumbled rocks slowly crept the Dragons—the littlest one coming first because he was hungry as well as angry.

The beasts had almost reached him when Woot, remembering his lace apron—now sadly torn and soiled—recovered his wits and shouted: "Open!" At the cry a hole appeared in the roof of the cavern, just over his head, and through it the sunlight streamed full upon the Green Monkey.

The Dragons paused, astonished at the magic and blinking at the sunlight, and this gave Woot time to climb through the opening. As soon as he reached the surface of the earth the hole closed again, and the boy monkey realized, with a thrill of joy, that he had seen the last of the dangerous Dragon family.

He sat upon the ground, still panting hard from his exertions, when the bushes before him parted and his former enemy, the Jaguar, appeared.

"Don't run," said the woodland beast, as Woot sprang up; "you are perfectly safe, so far as I am concerned, for since you so mysteriously disappeared I have had my breakfast. I am now on my way home, to sleep the rest of the day."

"Oh indeed!" returned the Green Monkey, in a tone both sorry and startled. "Which of my friends did you manage to eat?"

"None of them," returned the Jaguar, with a sly grin. "I had a dish of magic scrambled eggs —on toast—and it wasn't a bad feast, at all. There isn't room in me for even you, and I don't regret it because I judge, from your green color, that you are not ripe, and would make an indifferent meal. We jaguars have to be careful of our digestions. Farewell, Friend Monkey. Follow the path I made through the bushes and you will find your friends."

With this the Jaguar marched on his way and Woot took his advice and followed the trail he had made until he came to the place where the

little Brown Bear, and the Tin Owl, and the Canary were conferring together and wondering what had become of their comrade, the Green Monkey.

CHAPTER 10

"OUR best plan," said the Scarecrow Bear, when the Green Monkey had related the story of his adventure with the Dragons, "is to get out of this Gillikin Country as soon as we can and try to find our way to the castle of Glinda, the Good Sorceress. There are too many dangers lurking here to suit me, and Glinda may be able to restore us to our proper forms."

"If we turn south now," the Tin Owl replied, "we might go straight into the Emerald City. That's a place I wish to avoid, for I'd hate to have my friends see me in this sad plight," and he blinked his eyes and fluttered his tin wings mournfully.

"But I am certain we have passed *beyond* Emerald City," the Canary assured him, sailing lightly around their heads. "So, should we turn south from here, we would pass into the Munchkin Country, and continuing south we would reach the Quadling Country where Glinda's castle is located."

"Well, since you're sure of that, let's start right away," proposed the Bear. "It's a long journey, at the best, and I'm getting tired of walking on four legs."

"I thought you never tired, being stuffed with straw," said Woot.

"I mean that it annoys me, to be obliged to go on all fours, when two legs are my proper walking equipment," replied the Scarecrow. "I consider it beneath my dignity. In other words, my remarkable brains can tire, through humiliation, although my body cannot tire."

"That is one of the penalties of having brains," remarked the Tin Owl with a sigh. "I have had no brains since I was a man of meat, and so I never worry. Nevertheless, I prefer my former manly form to this owl's shape and would be glad to break Mrs. Yoop's enchantment as soon as possible. I am so noisy, just now, that I disturb myself," and he fluttered his wings with a clatter that echoed throughout the forest.

So, being all of one mind, they turned southward, traveling steadily on until the woods were left behind and the landscape turned from purple tints to blue tints, which assured them they had entered the Country of the Munchkins.

"Now I feel myself more safe," said the Scarecrow Bear. "I know this country pretty well, having been made here by a Munchkin farmer and having wandered over these lovely blue lands many times. Seems to me, indeed, that I even remember that group of three tall trees ahead of us; and, if I do, we are not far from the home of my friend Jinjur."

"Who is Jinjur?" asked Woot, the Green Monkey.

"Haven't you heard of Jinjur?" exclaimed the Scarecrow, in surprise.

"No," said Woot. "Is Jinjur a man, a woman, a beast or a bird?"

"Jinjur is a girl," explained the Scarecrow Bear. "She's a fine girl, too, although a bit restless and liable to get excited. Once, a long time ago, she raised an army of girls and called herself 'General Jinjur.' With her army she captured the Emerald City, and drove me out of it, because I insisted that an army in Oz was highly improper. But Ozma punished the rash girl, and afterward Jinjur and I became fast friends. Now Jinjur lives peacefully on a farm, near here, and raises fields of cream-puffs, chocolate-caramels and macaroons. They say she's a pretty good farmer, and in addition to that she's an artist, and paints pictures so perfect that one can scarcely tell them from nature. She often re-paints my face for me, when it gets worn or mussy, and the lovely expression I wore when the Giantess transformed me was painted by Jinjur only a month or so ago."

"It was certainly a pleasant expression," agreed Woot.

"Jinjur can paint anything," continued the Scarecrow Bear, with enthusiasm, as they walked along together. "Once, when I came to her house, my straw was old and crumpled, so that my body sagged dreadfully. I needed new straw to replace the old, but Jinjur had no straw on all her ranch and I was really unable to travel farther until I had been restuffed. When I ex-plained this to Jinjur, the girl at once painted a straw-stack which was so natural that I went to it and secured enough straw to fill all my body. It was a good quality of straw, too, and lasted me a long time."

This seemed very wonderful to Woot, who knew that such a thing could never happen in any place but a fairy country like Oz.

The Munchkin Country was much nicer than the Gillikin Country, and all the fields were separated by blue fences, with grassy lanes and paths of blue ground, and the land seemed well cultivated. They were on a little hill looking down upon this favored country, but had not quite reached the settled parts, when on turning a bend in the path they were halted by a form that barred their way.

A more curious creature they had seldom seen, even in the Land of Oz, where curious creatures abound. It had the head of a young man—evidently a Munchkin—with a pleasant face and hair neatly combed. But the body was very long, for it had twenty legs—ten legs on each side—and this caused the body to stretch out and lie in a horizontal position, so that all the legs could touch the ground and stand firm. From the shoulders extended two small arms; at least, they seemed small beside so many legs.

This odd creature was dressed in the regulation clothing of the Munchkin people, a dark blue coat neatly fitting the long body and each pair of legs having a pair of sky-blue trousers, with blue-tinted stockings and blue leather shoes turned up at the pointed toes.

"I wonder who you are?" said Polychrome the Canary, fluttering above the strange creature, who had probably been asleep on the path.

"I sometimes wonder, myself, who I am," replied the many-legged young man; "but, in reality, I am Tommy Kwikstep, and I live in a hollow tree that fell to the ground with age. I have polished the inside of it, and made a door

at each end, and that's a very comfortable residence for me because it just fits my shape."

"How did you happen to have such a shape?" asked the Scarecrow Bear, sitting on his haunches and regarding Tommy Kwikstep with a serious look. "Is the shape natural?"

"No; it was wished on me," replied Tommy, with a sigh. "I used to be very active and loved to run errands for anyone who needed my services. That was how I got my name of Tommy Kwikstep. I could run an errand more quickly than any other boy, and so I was very proud of myself. One day, however, I met an old lady who was a fairy, or a witch, or something of the sort, and she said if I would run an errand for her—to carry some magic medicine to another old woman—she would grant me just one Wish, whatever the Wish happened to be. Of course I consented and, taking the medicine, I hurried away. It was a long distance, mostly up hill, and my legs began to grow weary. Without thinking what I was doing I said aloud: 'Dear me; I wish I had twenty legs!' and in an instant I became the unusual creature you see beside you. Twenty legs! Twenty on one man! You may count them, if you doubt my word."

"You've got 'em, all right," said Woot the Monkey, who had already counted them.

"After I had delivered the magic medicine to the old woman, I returned and tried to find the witch, or fairy, or whatever she was, who had given me the unlucky wish, so she could take it away again. I've been searching for her ever since, but never can I find her," continued poor Tommy Kwikstep, sadly.

"I suppose," said the Tin Owl, blinking at him, "you can travel very fast, with those twenty legs."

"At first I was able to," was the reply; "but I traveled so much, searching for the fairy, or witch, or whatever she was, that I soon got corns on my toes. Now, a corn on one toe is not so bad, but when you have a hundred toes—as I have—and get corns on most of them, it is far from pleasant. Instead of running, I now painfully crawl, and although I try not to be discouraged I do hope I shall find that witch or fairy, or whatever she was, before long."

"I hope so, too," said the Scarecrow. "But, after all, you have the pleasure of knowing you are unusual, and therefore remarkable among the people of Oz. To be just like other persons is small credit to one, while to be unlike others is a mark of distinction."

"That *sounds* very pretty," returned Tommy Kwikstep, "but if you had to put on ten pair of trousers every morning, and tie up twenty shoes, you would prefer not to be so distinguished."

"Was the witch, or fairy, or whatever she was, an old person, with wrinkled skin and half her teeth gone?" inquired the Tin Owl.

"No," said Tommy Kwikstep.

"Then she wasn't Old Mombi," remarked the transformed Emperor.

"I'm not interested in who it *wasn't*, so much as I am in who it *was*," said the twenty-legged young man. "And, whatever or whomsoever she was, she has managed to keep out of my way."

"If you found her, do you suppose she'd change you back into a two-legged boy?" asked Woot.

"Perhaps so, if I could run another errand for her and so earn another wish."

"Would you really like to be as you were before?" asked Polychrome the Canary, perching upon the Green Monkey's shoulder to observe Tommy Kwikstep more attentively.

"I would, indeed," was the earnest reply.

"Then I will see what I can do for you," promised the Rainbow's Daughter, and flying to the ground she took a small twig in her bill and with it made several mystic figures on each side of Tommy Kwikstep.

"Are *you* a witch, or fairy, or something of the sort?" he asked as he watched her wonderingly.

The Canary made no answer, for she was busy, but the Scarecrow Bear replied: "Yes, she's something of the sort, and a bird of a magician."

The twenty-legged boy's transformation happened so queerly that they were all surprised at

its method. First, Tommy Kwikstep's last two legs disappeared; then the next two, and the next, and as each pair of legs vanished his body shortened. All this while Polychrome was running around him and chirping mystical words, and when all the young man's legs had disappeared but two he noticed that the Canary was still busy and cried out in alarm:

"Stop—stop! Leave me *two* of my legs, or I shall be worse off than before."

"I know," said the Canary. "I'm only removing with my magic the corns from your last ten toes."

"Thank you for being so thoughtful," he said gratefully, and now they noticed that Tommy Kwikstep was quite a nice-looking young fellow.

"What will you do now?" asked Woot the Monkey.

"First," he answered, "I must deliver a note which I've carried in my pocket ever since the witch, or fairy, or whatever she was, granted my foolish wish. And I am resolved never to speak again without taking time to think carefully on what I am going to say, for I realize that speech without thought is dangerous. And after I've delivered the note, I shall run errands again for anyone who needs my services."

So he thanked Polychrome again and started away in a different direction from their own, and that was the last they saw of Tommy Kwikstep.

Jinjur's Ranch

CHAPTER 11

AS they followed a path down the blue-grass hillside, the first house that met the view of the travelers was joyously recognized by the Scarecrow Bear as the one inhabited by his friend Jinjur, so they increased their speed and hurried toward it.

On reaching the place, however, they found the house deserted. The front door stood open, but no one was inside. In the garden surrounding the house were neat rows of bushes bearing cream-puffs and macaroons, some of which were still green, but others ripe and ready to eat. Farther back were fields of caramels, and all the land seemed well cultivated and carefully tended. They looked through the fields for the girl farmer, but she was nowhere to be seen.

"Well," finally remarked the little Brown Bear, "let us go into the house and make ourselves at home. That will be sure to please my friend Jinjur, who happens to be away from home just now. When she returns, she will be greatly surprised."

"Would she care if I ate some of those ripe cream-puffs?" asked the Green Monkey.

"No, indeed; Jinjur is very generous. Help yourself to all you want," said the Scarecrow Bear.

So Woot gathered a lot of the cream-puffs that were golden yellow and filled with a sweet, creamy substance, and ate until his hunger was satisfied. Then he entered the house with his friends and sat in a rocking-chair—just as he was accustomed to do when a boy. The Canary perched herself upon the mantel and daintily plumed her feathers; the Tin Owl sat on the back of another chair; the Scarecrow squatted on his hairy haunches in the middle of the room.

"I believe I remember the girl Jinjur," remarked the Canary, in her sweet voice. "She cannot help us very much, except to direct us on our way to Glinda's castle, for she does not understand magic. But she's a good girl, honest and sensible, and I'll be glad to see her."

"All our troubles," said the Owl with a deep sigh, "arose from my foolish resolve to seek Nimmie Amee and make her Empress of the Winkies, and while I wish to reproach no one, I must say that it was Woot the Wanderer who put the notion into my head."

"Well, for my part, I am glad he did," responded the Canary. "Your journey resulted in saving me from the Giantess, and had you not traveled to the Yoop Valley, I would still be Mrs. Yoop's prisoner. It is much nicer to be free, even though I still bear the enchanted form of a Canary-Bird."

"Do you think we shall ever be able to get our proper forms back again?" asked the Green Monkey earnestly.

Polychrome did not make reply at once to this important question, but after a period of thoughtfulness she said:

"I have been taught to believe that there is an antidote for every magic charm, yet Mrs. Yoop insists that no power can alter her transformations. I realize that my own fairy magic cannot do it, although I have thought that we Sky Fairies have more power than is accorded to Earth Fairies. The yookoohoo magic is admitted to be very strange in its workings and different from the magic usually practiced, but perhaps Glinda or Ozma may understand it better than I. In them lies our only hope. Unless they can help us, we must remain forever as we are."

"A Canary-Bird on a Rainbow wouldn't be so bad," asserted the Tin Owl, winking and blinking with his round tin eyes, "so if you can manage to find your Rainbow again you need have little to worry about."

"That's nonsense, Friend Chopper," exclaimed Woot. "I know just how Polychrome feels. A beautiful girl is much superior to a little yellow bird, and a boy—such as I was—far better than a Green Monkey. Neither of us can be happy again unless we recover our rightful forms."

"I feel the same way," announced the stuffed Bear. "What do you suppose my friend the Patchwork Girl would think of me, if she saw me wearing this beastly shape?"

"She'd laugh till she cried," admitted the Tin Owl. "For my part, I'll have to give up the notion of marrying Nimmie Amee, but I'll try not to let that make me unhappy. If it's my duty, I'd like to do my duty, but if magic prevents my getting married I'll flutter along all by myself and be just as contented."

Their serious misfortunes made them all silent for a time, and as their thoughts were busy in dwelling upon the evils with which fate had burdened them, none noticed that Jinjur had suddenly appeared in the doorway and was looking at them in astonishment. The next moment her astonishment changed to anger, for there, in her best rocking-chair, sat a Green Monkey. A great shiny Owl perched upon another chair and a Brown Bear squatted upon her parlor rug. Jinjur did not notice the Canary, but she caught up a broomstick and dashed into the room, shouting as she came:

"Get out of here, you wild creatures! How dare you enter my house?"

With a blow of her broom she knocked the Brown Bear over, and the Tin Owl tried to fly out of her reach and made a great clatter with his tin wings. The Green Monkey was so startled by the sudden attack that he sprang into the fireplace—where there was fortunately no fire— and tried to escape by climbing up the chimney. But he found the opening too small, and so was forced to drop down again. Then he crouched trembling in the fireplace, his pretty green hair all blackened with soot and covered with ashes. From this position Woot watched to see what would happen next.

"Stop, Jinjur—stop!" cried the Brown Bear, when the broom again threatened him. "Don't you know me? I'm your old friend the Scarecrow!"

"You're trying to deceive me, you naughty beast! I can see plainly that you are a bear, and a mighty poor specimen of a bear, too," retorted the girl.

"That's because I'm not properly stuffed," he assured her. "When Mrs. Yoop transformed me, she didn't realize I should have more stuffing."

"Who is Mrs. Yoop?" inquired Jinjur, pausing with the broom still upraised.

"A Giantess in the Gillikin Country."

"Oh; I begin to understand. And Mrs. Yoop transformed you? You are really the famous Scarecrow of Oz?"

"I *was*, Jinjur. Just now I'm as you see me—a miserable little Brown Bear with a poor quality of stuffing. That Tin Owl is none other than our dear Tin Woodman—Nick Chopper, the Emperor of the Winkies—while this Green Monkey is a nice little boy we recently became acquainted with, Woot the Wanderer."

"And I," said the Canary, flying close to Jinjur, "am Polychrome, the Daughter of the Rainbow, in the form of a bird."

"Goodness me!" cried Jinjur, amazed; "that Giantess must be a powerful Sorceress, and as wicked as she is powerful."

"She's a yookoohoo," said Polychrome. "Fortunately, we managed to escape from her castle, and we are now on our way to Glinda the Good to see if she possesses the power to restore us to our former shapes."

"Then I must beg your pardons; all of you must forgive me," said Jinjur, putting away the broom. "I took you to be a lot of wild, unmannerly animals, as was quite natural. You are very welcome to my home and I'm sorry I haven't the power to help you out of your troubles. Please use my house and all that I have, as if it were your own."

At this declaration of peace, the Bear got upon his feet and the Owl resumed his perch upon the chair and the Monkey crept out of the fireplace. Jinjur looked at Woot critically, and scowled.

"For a Green Monkey," said she, "you're the blackest creature I ever saw. And you'll get my nice clean room all dirty with soot and ashes. Whatever possessed you to jump up the chimney?"

"I—I was scared," explained Woot, somewhat ashamed.

"Well, you need renovating, and that's what will happen to you, right away. Come with me!" she commanded.

"What are you going to do?" asked Woot.

"Give you a good scrubbing," said Jinjur.

Now, neither boys nor monkeys relish being scrubbed, so Woot shrank away from the energetic girl, trembling fearfully. But Jinjur grabbed him by his paw and dragged him out to the back yard, where, in spite of his whines and struggles, she plunged him into a tub of cold water and began to scrub him with a stiff brush and a cake of yellow soap.

This was the hardest trial that Woot had endured since he became a monkey, but no protest had any influence with Jinjur, who lathered and scrubbed him in a business-like manner and afterward dried him with a coarse towel.

The Bear and the Owl gravely watched this operation and nodded approval when Woot's silky green fur shone clear and bright in the afternoon sun. The Canary seemed much amused and laughed a silvery ripple of laughter as she said:

"Very well done, my good Jinjur; I admire your energy and judgment. But I had no idea a monkey could look so comical as this monkey did while he was being bathed."

"I'm *not* a monkey!" declared Woot, resentfully; "I'm just a boy in a monkey's shape, that's all."

"If you can explain to me the difference," said Jinjur, "I'll agree not to wash you again—

that is, unless you foolishly get into the fireplace. All persons are usually judged by the shapes in which they appear to the eyes of others. Look at *me*, Woot; what am *I?*"

Woot looked at her.

"You're as pretty a girl as I've ever seen," he replied.

Jinjur frowned. That is, she tried hard to frown.

"Come out into the garden with me," she said, "and I'll give you some of the most delicious caramels you ever ate. They're a new variety, that no one can grow but me, and they have a heliotrope flavor."

Ozma and Dorothy

CHAPTER 12

IN her magnificent palace in the Emerald City, the beautiful girl Ruler of all the wonderful Land of Oz sat in her dainty boudoir with her friend Princess Dorothy beside her. Ozma was studying a roll of manuscript which she had taken from the Royal Library, while Dorothy worked at her embroidery and at times stooped to pat a shaggy little black dog that lay at her feet. The little dog's name was Toto, and he was Dorothy's faithful companion.

To judge Ozma of Oz by the standards of our world, you would think her very young—perhaps fourteen or fifteen years of age—yet for years she had ruled the Land of Oz and had never seemed a bit older. Dorothy appeared much younger than Ozma. She had been a little girl when first she came to the Land of Oz, and she was a little girl still, and would never seem to be a day older while she lived in this wonderful fairyland.

Oz was not always a fairyland, I am told. Once it was much like other lands, except it was shut in by a dreadful desert of sandy wastes that lay all around it, thus preventing its people from all contact with the rest of the world. Seeing this isolation, the fairy band of Queen Lurline, passing over Oz while on a journey, enchanted the country and so made it a Fairyland. And Queen Lurline left one of her fairies to rule this enchanted Land of Oz, and then passed on and forgot all about it.

From that moment no one in Oz ever died. Those who were old remained old; those who were young and strong did not change as years passed them by; the children remained children always, and played and romped to their hearts' content, while all the babies lived in their cradles and were tenderly cared for and never grew up. So people in Oz stopped counting how old they were in years, for years made no difference in their appearance and could not alter their station. They did not get sick, so there were no doctors among them. Accidents might happen to some, on rare occasions, it is true, and while no one could die naturally, as other people do, it was possible that one might be totally destroyed. Such incidents, however, were very unusual, and so seldom was there anything to worry over that the Oz people were as happy and contented as can be.

Another strange thing about this fairy Land of Oz was that whoever managed to enter it from the outside world came under the magic spell of the place and did not change in appearance as long as they lived there. So Dorothy, who now lived with Ozma, seemed just the same sweet little girl she had been when first she came to this delightful fairyland.

Perhaps all parts of Oz might not be called truly delightful, but it was surely delightful in the neighborhood of the Emerald City, where Ozma reigned. Her loving influence was felt for many miles around, but there were places in the mountains of the Gillikin Country, and the forests of the Quadling Country, and perhaps in far-away parts of the Munchkin and Winkie Countries, where the inhabitants were somewhat rude and uncivilized and had not yet come under the spell of Ozma's wise and kindly rule. Also, when Oz first became a fairyland, it harbored several witches and magicians and sorcerers and necromancers, who were scattered in various parts, but most of these had been deprived of their magic powers, and Ozma had issued a royal edict forbidding anyone in her dominions to work magic except Glinda the Good and the Wizard of Oz. Ozma herself, being a real fairy, knew a lot of magic, but she only used it to benefit her subjects.

This little explanation will help you to understand better the story you are reading, but most of it is already known to those who are familiar with the Oz people whose adventures they have followed in other Oz books.

Ozma and Dorothy were fast friends and were much together. Everyone in Oz loved Dorothy almost as well as they did their lovely Ruler, for the little Kansas girl's good fortune had not spoiled her or rendered her at all vain. She was just the same brave and true and adventurous child as before she lived in a royal palace and became the chum of the fairy Ozma.

In the room in which the two sat—which was one of Ozma's private suite of apartments—hung the famous Magic Picture. This was the source of constant interest to little Dorothy. One had but to stand before it and wish to see what any person was doing, and at once a scene would flash upon the magic canvas which showed exactly where that person was, and like our own moving pictures would reproduce the actions of that person as long as you cared to watch them. So today, when Dorothy tired of her embroidery, she drew the curtains from before the Magic Picture and wished to see what her friend Button Bright was doing. Button Bright, she saw, was playing ball with Ojo, the Munchkin boy, so Dorothy next wished to see what her Aunt Em was doing. The picture showed Aunt Em quietly engaged in darning socks for Uncle Henry, so Dorothy wished to see what her old friend the Tin Woodman was doing.

The Tin Woodman was then just leaving his tin castle in the company of the Scarecrow and Woot the Wanderer. Dorothy had never seen this boy before, so she wondered who he was. Also she was curious to know where the three were going, for she noticed Woot's knapsack and guessed they had started on a long journey. She asked Ozma about it, but Ozma did not know.

That afternoon Dorothy again saw the travelers in the Magic Picture, but they were merely tramping through the country and Dorothy was not much interested in them. A couple of days later, however, the girl, being again with Ozma, wished to see her friends, the Scarecrow and the Tin Woodman in the Magic Picture, and on this occasion found them in the great castle of Mrs. Yoop, the Giantess, who was at the time about to transform them. Both Dorothy and

Ozma now became greatly interested and watched the transformations with indignation and horror.

"What a wicked Giantess!" exclaimed Dorothy.

"Yes," answered Ozma, "she must be punished for this cruelty to our friends, and to the poor boy who is with them."

After this they followed the adventure of the little Brown Bear and the Tin Owl and the Green Monkey with breathless interest, and were delighted when they escaped from Mrs. Yoop. They did not know, then, who the Canary was, but realized it must be the transformation of some person of consequence, whom the Giantess had also enchanted.

When, finally, the day came when the adventurers headed south into the Munchkin

Country, Dorothy asked anxiously:

"Can't something be done for them, Ozma? Can't you change 'em back into their own shapes? They've suffered enough from these dreadful transformations, seems to me."

"I've been studying ways to help them, ever since they were transformed," replied Ozma. "Mrs. Yoop is now the only yookoohoo in my dominions, and the yookoohoo magic is very peculiar and hard for others to understand, yet I am resolved to make the attempt to break these enchantments. I may not succeed, but I shall do the best I can. From the directions our friends are taking, I believe they are going to pass by Jinjur's Ranch, so if we start now we may meet them there. Would you like to go with me, Dorothy?"

"Of course," answered the little girl; "I wouldn't miss it for anything."

"Then order the Red Wagon," said Ozma of Oz, "and we will start at once."

Dorothy ran to do as she was bid, while Ozma went to her Magic Room to make ready the things she believed she would need. In half an hour the Red Wagon stood before the grand entrance of the palace, and before it was hitched the Wooden Sawhorse, which was Ozma's favorite steed.

This Sawhorse, while made of wood, was very much alive and could travel swiftly and

without tiring. To keep the ends of his wooden legs from wearing down short, Ozma had shod the Sawhorse with plates of pure gold. His harness was studded with brilliant emeralds and other jewels and so, while he himself was not at all handsome, his outfit made a splendid appearance.

Since the Sawhorse could understand her spoken words, Ozma used no reins to guide him. She merely told him where to go. When she came from the palace with Dorothy, they both climbed into the Red Wagon and then the little dog, Toto, ran up and asked:

"Are you going to leave me behind, Dorothy?"

Dorothy looked at Ozma, who smiled in return and said:

"Toto may go with us, if you wish him to."

So Dorothy lifted the little dog into the wagon, for, while he could run fast, he could not keep up with the speed of the wonderful Sawhorse.

Away they went, over hills and through meadows, covering the ground with astonishing speed. It is not surprising, therefore, that the Red Wagon arrived before Jinjur's house just as that energetic young lady had finished scrubbing the Green Monkey and was about to lead him to the caramel patch.

The Restoration

CHAPTER 13

THE Tin Owl gave a hoot of delight when he saw the Red Wagon draw up before Jinjur's house, and the Brown Bear grunted and growled with glee and trotted toward Ozma as fast as he could wobble. As for the Canary, it flew swiftly to Dorothy's shoulder and perched there, saying in in her ear:

"Thank goodness you have come to our rescue!"

"But who are you?" asked Dorothy.

"Don't you know?" returned the Canary.

"No; for the first time we noticed you in the Magic Picture, you were just a bird, as you are now. But we've guessed that the giant woman had transformed you, as she did the others."

"Yes; I'm Polychrome, the Rainbow's Daughter," announced the Canary.

"Goodness me!" cried Dorothy. "How dreadful."

"Well, I make a rather pretty bird, I think," returned Polychrome, "but of course I'm anxious to resume my own shape and get back upon my rainbow."

"Ozma will help you, I'm sure," said Dorothy. "How does it feel, Scarecrow, to be a Bear?" she asked, addressing her old friend.

"I don't like it," declared the Scarecrow Bear. "This brutal form is quite beneath the dignity of a wholesome straw man."

"And think of me," said the Owl, perching upon the dashboard of the Red Wagon with much noisy clattering of his tin feathers. "Don't I look horrid, Dorothy, with eyes several sizes too big for my body, and so weak that I ought to wear spectacles?"

"Well," said Dorothy critically, as she looked him over, "you're nothing to brag of, I must confess. But Ozma will soon fix you up again."

The Green Monkey had hung back, bashful at meeting two lovely girls while in the form of a beast; but Jinjur now took his hand and led him forward while she introduced him to Ozma, and Woot managed to make a low bow, not really ungraceful, before her girlish Majesty, the Ruler of Oz.

"You have all been forced to endure a sad experience," said Ozma, "and so I am anxious to do all in my power to break Mrs. Yoop's enchantments. But first tell me how you happened to stray into that lonely Valley where Yoop Castle stands."

Between them they related the object of their journey, the Scarecrow Bear telling of the Tin Woodman's resolve to find Nimmie Amee and marry her, as a just reward for her loyalty to him. Woot told of their adventures with the Loons of Loonville, and the Tin Owl described the manner in which they had been captured and transformed by the Giantess. Then Polychrome related her story, and when all had been told, and Dorothy had several times reproved Toto for growling at the Tin Owl, Ozma remained thoughtful for a while, pondering upon what she had heard. Finally she looked up, and with one of her delightful smiles, said to the anxious group:

"I am not sure my magic will be able to restore every one of you, because your transformations are of such a strange and unusual character. Indeed, Mrs. Yoop was quite justified in believing no power could alter her enchantments. However, I am sure I can restore the Scarecrow to his original shape. He was stuffed with straw from the beginning, and even the yookoohoo magic could not alter that. The Giantess was merely able to make a bear's shape of a man's shape, but the bear is stuffed with straw, just as the man was. So I feel confident I can make a man of the bear again."

"Hurrah!" cried the Brown Bear, and tried clumsily to dance a jig of delight.

"As for the Tin Woodman, his case is much the same," resumed Ozma, still smiling. "The power of the Giantess could not make him anything but a tin creature, whatever shape she transformed him into, so it will not be impossible to restore him to his manly form. Anyhow, I shall test my magic at once, and see if it will do what I have promised."

She drew from her bosom a small silver Wand and, making passes with the Wand over the head of the Bear, she succeeded in the brief space of a moment in breaking his enchantment. The original Scarecrow of Oz again stood before them, well stuffed with straw and with his features nicely painted upon the bag which formed his head.

The Scarecrow was greatly delighted, as you may suppose, and he strutted proudly around while the powerful fairy, Ozma of Oz, broke the enchantment that had transformed the Tin Woodman and made a Tin Owl into a Tin Man again.

"Now, then," chirped the Canary, eagerly; "I'm next, Ozma!"

"But your case is different," replied Ozma, no longer smiling but wearing a grave expression on her sweet face. "I shall have to experiment on you, Polychrome, and I may fail in all my attempts."

She then tried two or three different methods of magic, hoping one of them would succeed in breaking Polychrome's enchantment, but still the Rainbow's Daughter remained a Canary-Bird. Finally, however, she experimented in another way. She transformed the Canary into a Dove, and then transformed the Dove into a Speckled Hen, and then changed the Speckled Hen into a rabbit, and then the rabbit into a Fawn. And at the last, after mixing several powders and sprinkling them upon the Fawn, the yookoohoo enchantment was suddenly broken and before them stood one of the daintiest and loveliest creatures in any fairyland in the world. Polychrome was as sweet and merry in disposition as she was beautiful, and when she danced and capered around in delight, her beautiful hair floated around her like a golden mist and her many-hued raiment, as soft as cobwebs, reminded one of drifting clouds in a summer sky.

Woot was so awed by the entrancing sight of this exquisite Sky Fairy that he quite forgot his own sad plight until he noticed Ozma gazing upon him with an intent expression that denoted sympathy and sorrow. Dorothy whispered in her friend's ear, but the Ruler of Oz shook her head sadly.

Jinjur, noticing this and understanding Ozma's looks, took the paw of the Green Monkey in her own hand and patted it softly.

"Never mind," she said to him. "You are a very beautiful color, and a monkey can climb better than a boy and do a lot of other things no boy can ever do."

"What's the matter?" asked Woot, a sinking feeling at his heart. "Is Ozma's magic all used up?"

Ozma herself answered him.

"Your form of enchantment, my poor boy," she said pityingly, "is different from that of the others. Indeed, it is a form that is impossible to alter by any magic known to fairies or yookoohoos. The wicked Giantess was well aware, when she gave you the form of a Green Monkey, that the Green Monkey must exist in the Land of Oz for all future time."

Woot drew a long sigh.

"Well, that's pretty hard luck," he said bravely, "but if it can't be helped I must endure it; that's all. I don't like being a monkey, but what's the use of kicking against my fate?"

They were all very sorry for him, and Dorothy anxiously asked Ozma:

"Couldn't Glinda save him?"

"No," was the reply. "Glinda's power in transformations is no greater than my own. Before I left my palace I went to my Magic Room and studied Woot's case very carefully. I found that no power can do away with the Green Monkey. He might transfer, or exchange his form with some other person, it is true; but the Green Monkey we cannot get rid of by any magic arts known to science."

"But—see here," said the Scarecrow, who had listened intently to this explanation, "why not put the monkey's form on someone else?"

"Who would agree to make the change?" asked Ozma. "If by force we caused anyone else to become a Green Monkey, we would be as cruel and wicked as Mrs. Yoop. And what good would an exchange do?" she continued. "Suppose, for instance, we worked the enchantment, and made Toto into a Green Monkey. At the same moment Woot would become a little dog."

"Leave me out of your magic, please," said Toto, with a reproachful growl. "I wouldn't become a Green Monkey for anything."

"And I wouldn't become a dog," said Woot. "A green monkey is much better than a dog, it seems to me."

"That is only a matter of opinion," answered Toto.

"Now, here's another idea," said the Scarecrow. "My brains are working finely today, you must admit. Why not transform Toto into Woot the Wanderer, and then have them exchange forms? The dog would become a green monkey and the monkey would have his own natural shape again."

"To be sure!" cried Jinjur. "That's a fine idea."

"Leave me out of it," said Toto. "I won't do it."

"Wouldn't you be willing to become a green monkey—see what a pretty color it is—so that this poor boy could be restored to his own shape?" asked Jinjur, pleadingly.

"No," said Toto.

"I don't like that plan the least bit," declared Dorothy, "for then I wouldn't have any little dog."

"But you'd have a green monkey in his place," persisted Jinjur, who liked Woot and wanted to help him.

"I don't want a green monkey," said Dorothy positively.

"Don't speak of this again, I beg of you," said Woot. "This is my own misfortune and I would rather suffer it alone than deprive Princess Dorothy of her dog, or deprive the dog of his proper shape. And perhaps even her Majesty, Ozma of Oz, might not be able to transform anyone else into the shape of Woot the Wanderer."

"Yes; I believe I might do that," Ozma returned; "but Woot is quite right; we are not justified in inflicting upon anyone—man or dog— the form of a green monkey. Also it is certain that in order to relieve the boy of the form he now wears, we must give it to someone else, who would be forced to wear it always."

"I wonder," said Dorothy, thoughtfully, "if we couldn't find someone in the Land of Oz who would be willing to become a green monkey? Seems to me a monkey is active and spry, and he can climb trees and do a lot of clever things, and green isn't a bad color for a monkey —it makes him unusual."

"I wouldn't ask anyone to take this dreadful form," said Woot; "it wouldn't be right, you know. I've been a monkey for some time, now, and I don't like it. It makes me ashamed to be a beast of this sort when by right of birth I'm a boy; so I'm sure it would be wicked to ask anyone else to take my place."

They were all silent, for they knew he spoke the truth. Dorothy was almost ready to cry with pity and Ozma's sweet face was sad and disturbed. The Scarecrow rubbed and patted his stuffed head to try to make it think better, while the Tin Woodman went into the house and began to oil his tin joints so that the sorrow of his friends might not cause him to weep. Weeping is liable to rust tin, and the Emperor prided himself upon his highly polished body—now

doubly dear to him because for a time he had been deprived of it.

Polychrome had danced down the garden paths and back again a dozen times, for she was seldom still a moment, yet she had heard Ozma's speech and understood very well Woot's unfortunate position. But the Rainbow's Daughter, even while dancing, could think and reason very clearly, and suddenly she solved the problem in the nicest possible way. Coming close to Ozma, she said:

"Your Majesty, all this trouble was caused by the wickedness of Mrs. Yoop, the Giantess. Yet even now that cruel woman is living in her secluded castle, enjoying the thought that she has put this terrible enchantment on Woot the Wanderer. Even now she is laughing at our despair because we can find no way to get rid of the green monkey. Very well, we do not wish to get rid of it. Let the woman who created the form wear it herself, as a just punishment for her wickedness. I am sure your fairy power can give to Mrs. Yoop the form of Woot the Wanderer— even at this distance from her—and then it will be possible to exchange the two forms. Mrs. Yoop will become the Green Monkey, and Woot will recover his own form again."

Ozma's face brightened as she listened to this clever proposal.

"Thank you, Polychrome," said she. "The

task you propose is not so easy as you suppose, but I will make the attempt, and perhaps I may succeed."

The Green Monkey

CHAPTER 14

THEY now entered the house, and as an interested group, watched Jinjur, at Ozma's command, build a fire and put a kettle of water over to boil. The Ruler of Oz stood before the fire silent and grave, while the others, realizing that an important ceremony of magic was about to be performed, stood quietly in the background so as not to interrupt Ozma's proceedings. Only Polychrome kept going in and coming out, humming softly to herself as she danced, for the Rainbow's Daughter could not keep still for long, and the four walls of a room always made her nervous and ill at ease. She moved so noiselessly, however, that her movements were like the shifting of sunbeams and did not annoy anyone.

When the water in the kettle bubbled, Ozma drew from her bosom two tiny packets containing powders. These powders she threw into the kettle and after briskly stirring the contents with a branch from a macaroon bush, Ozma poured the mystic broth upon a broad platter which Jinjur had placed upon the table. As the broth cooled it became as silver, reflecting all objects from its smooth surface like a mirror.

While her companions gathered around the table, eagerly attentive—and Dorothy even held little Toto in her arms that he might see—Ozma waved her wand over the mirror-like surface. At once it reflected the interior of Yoop Castle, and in the big hall sat Mrs. Yoop, in her best embroidered silken robes, engaged in weaving a new lace apron to replace the one she had lost.

The Giantess seemed rather uneasy, as if she had a faint idea that someone was spying upon her, for she kept looking behind her and this way and that, as though expecting danger from an unknown source. Perhaps some yookoohoo instinct warned her. Woot saw that she had escaped from her room by some of the magical means at her disposal, after her prisoners had escaped her. She was now occupying the big hall

of her castle as she used to do. Also Woot thought, from the cruel expression on the face of the Giantess, that she was planning revenge on them, as soon as her new magic apron was finished.

But Ozma was now making passes over the platter with her silver Wand, and presently the form of the Giantess began to shrink in size and to change its shape. And now in her place sat the form of Woot the Wanderer, and as if suddenly realizing her transformation Mrs. Yoop threw down her work and rushed to a looking-glass that stood against the wall of her room. When she saw the boy's form reflected as her own, she grew violently angry and dashed her head against the mirror, smashing it to atoms.

Just then Ozma was busy with her magic Wand, making strange figures, and she had also placed her left hand firmly upon the shoulder of the Green Monkey. So now, as all eyes were turned upon the platter, the form of Mrs. Yoop gradually changed again. She was slowly transformed into the Green Monkey, and at the same time Woot slowly regained his natural form.

It was quite a surprise to them all when they raised their eyes from the platter and saw Woot the Wanderer standing beside Ozma. And, when they glanced at the platter again, it reflected nothing more than the walls of the room in Jinjur's house in which they stood. The magic ceremonial was ended, and Ozma of Oz had triumphed over the wicked Giantess.

"What will become of her, I wonder?" said Dorothy, as she drew a long breath.

"She will always remain a Green Monkey," replied Ozma, "and in that form she will be unable to perform any magical arts whatsoever. She need not be unhappy, however, and as she lives all alone in her castle she probably won't mind the transformation very much after she gets used to it."

"Anyhow, it serves her right," declared Dorothy, and all agreed with her.

"But," said the kind-hearted Tin Woodman, "I'm afraid the Green Monkey will starve, for Mrs. Yoop used to get her food by magic, and now that the magic is taken away from her, what can she eat?"

"Why, she'll eat what other monkeys do," returned the Scarecrow. "Even in the form of a Green Monkey, she's a very clever person, and I'm sure her wits will show her how to get plenty to eat."

"Don't worry about her," advised Dorothy. "She didn't worry about you, and her condition is no worse than the condition she imposed on poor Woot. She can't starve *to death* in the Land of Oz, that's certain, and if she gets hungry at times it's no more than the wicked thing deserves. Let's forget Mrs. Yoop; for, in spite of her being a yookoohoo, our fairy friends have broken all of her transformations."

The Man of Tin

CHAPTER 15

OZMA and Dorothy were quite pleased with Woot the Wanderer, whom they found modest and intelligent and very well mannered. The boy was truly grateful for his release from the cruel enchantment, and he promised to love, revere and defend the girl Ruler of Oz forever afterward, as a faithful subject.

"You may visit me at my palace, if you wish," said Ozma, "where I will be glad to introduce you to two other nice boys, Ojo the Munchkin and Button-Bright."

"Thank your Majesty," replied Woot, and then he turned to the Tin Woodman and inquired: "What are your further plans, Mr. Emperor? Will you still seek Nimmie Amee and marry her, or will you abandon the quest and return to the Emerald City and your own castle?"

The Tin Woodman, now as highly polished and well-oiled as ever, reflected a while on this question and then answered:

"Well, I see no reason why I should not find Nimmie Amee. We are now in the Munchkin Country, where we are perfectly safe, and if it was right for me, before our enchantment, to marry Nimmie Amee and make her Empress of the Winkies, it must be right now, when the enchantment has been broken and I am once more myself. Am I correct, friend Scarecrow?"

"You are, indeed," answered the Scarecrow. "No one can oppose such logic."

"But I'm afraid you don't love Nimmie Amee," suggested Dorothy.

"That is just because I can't love anyone," replied the Tin Woodman. "But, if I cannot love my wife, I can at least be kind to her, and all husbands are not able to do that."

"Do you s'pose Nimmie Amee still loves you, after all these years?" asked Dorothy.

"I'm quite sure of it, and that is why I am going to her to make her happy. Woot the Wanderer thinks I ought to reward her for being faithful to me after my meat body was chopped to pieces and I became tin. What do *you* think, Ozma?"

Ozma smiled as she said:

"I do not know your Nimmie Amee, and so I cannot tell what she most needs to make her happy. But there is no harm in your going to her and asking her if she still wishes to marry you. If she does, we will give you a grand wedding at the Emerald City and, afterward, as Empress of the Winkies, Nimmie Amee would become one of the most important ladies in all Oz."

So it was decided that the Tin Woodman would continue his journey, and that the Scarecrow and Woot the Wanderer should accompany him, as before. Polychrome also decided to join their party, somewhat to the surprise of all.

"I hate to be cooped up in a palace," she said to Ozma, "and of course the first time I meet my Rainbow I shall return to my own dear home in the skies, where my fairy sisters are even now awaiting me and my father is cross because I get lost so often. But I can find my Rainbow just as quickly while traveling in the Munchkin Country as I could if living in the Emerald City—or any other place in Oz—so I shall go with the Tin Woodman and help him woo Nimmie Amee."

Dorothy wanted to go, too, but as the Tin Woodman did not invite her to join his party, she felt she might be intruding if she asked to be taken. She hinted, but she found he didn't take the hint. It is quite a delicate matter for one to ask a girl to marry him, however much she loves him, and perhaps the Tin Woodman did not desire to have too many looking on when he found his old sweetheart, Nimmie Amee. So Dorothy contented herself with the thought that she would help Ozma prepare a splendid wedding feast, to be followed by a round of parties and festivities when the Emperor of the Winkies reached the Emerald City with his bride.

Ozma offered to take them all in the Red Wagon to a place as near to the great Munchkin forest as a wagon could get. The Red Wagon was big enough to seat them all, and so, bidding good-bye to Jinjur, who gave Woot a basket of ripe cream-puffs and caramels to take with him, Ozma commanded the Wooden Sawhorse to start, and the strange creature moved swiftly over the lanes and presently came to the Road of Yellow Bricks. This road led straight to a dense forest, where the path was too narrow for the Red Wagon to proceed farther, so here the party separated.

Ozma and Dorothy and Toto returned to the Emerald City, after wishing their friends a safe and successful journey, while the Tin Woodman, the Scarecrow, Woot the Wanderer and Polychrome, the Rainbow's Daughter, prepared to push their way through the thick forest. However, these forest paths were well known to the Tin Man and the Scarecrow, who felt quite at home among the trees.

"I was born in this grand forest," said Nick Chopper, the tin Emperor, speaking proudly, "and it was here that the Witch enchanted my axe and I lost different parts of my meat body until I became all tin. Here, also—for it is a big forest—Nimmie Amee lived with the Wicked Witch, and at the other edge of the trees stands the cottage of my friend Ku-Klip, the famous tinsmith who made my present beautiful form."

"He must be a clever workman," declared Woot, admiringly.

"He is simply wonderful," declared the Tin Woodman.

"I shall be glad to make his acquaintance," said Woot.

"If you wish to meet with real cleverness," remarked the Scarecrow, "you should visit the Munchkin farmer who first made *me*. I won't say that my friend the Emperor isn't all right for a tin man, but any judge of beauty can understand that a Scarecrow is far more artistic and refined."

"You are too soft and flimsy," said the Tin Woodman.

"You are too hard and stiff," said the Scarecrow, and this was as near to quarreling as the two friends ever came. Polychrome laughed at them both, as well she might, and Woot hastened to change the subject.

At night they all camped underneath the trees. The boy ate cream-puffs for supper and offered Polychrome some, but she preferred other food and at daybreak sipped the dew that was clustered thick on the forest flowers. Then they tramped onward again, and presently the Scarecrow paused and said:

"It was on this very spot that Dorothy and I first met the Tin Woodman, who was rusted so badly that none of his joints would move. But after we had oiled him up, he was as good as new and accompanied us to the Emerald City."

"Ah, that was a sad experience," asserted the Tin Woodman soberly. "I was caught in a rainstorm while chopping down a tree for exercise, and before I realized it, I was firmly rusted in every joint. There I stood, axe in hand, but unable to move, for days and weeks and months! Indeed, I have never known exactly how long the time was; but finally along came Dorothy and I was saved. See! This is the very tree I was chopping at the time I rusted."

"You cannot be far from your old home, in that case," said Woot.

"No; my little cabin stands not a great way off, but there is no occasion for us to visit it. Our errand is with Nimmie Amee, and her house is somewhat farther away, to the left of us."

"Didn't you say she lives with a Wicked Witch, who makes her a slave?" asked the boy.

"She did, but she doesn't," was the reply. "I am told the Witch was destroyed when Dorothy's house fell on her, so now Nimmie Amee must live all alone. I haven't seen her, of course, since the Witch was crushed, for at that time I was standing rusted in the forest and had been there a long time, but the poor girl must have felt very happy to be free from her cruel mistress."

"Well," said the Scarecrow, "let's travel on and find Nimmie Amee. Lead on, your Majesty, since you know the way, and we will follow."

So the Tin Woodman took a path that led through the thickest part of the forest, and they followed it for some time. The light was dim here, because vines and bushes and leafy foliage were all about them, and often the Tin Man had to push aside the branches that obstructed their way, or cut them off with his axe. After they had proceeded some distance, the Emperor suddenly stopped short and exclaimed: "Good gracious!"

The Scarecrow, who was next, first bumped into his friend and then peered around his tin body, and said in a tone of wonder:

"Well, I declare!"

Woot the Wanderer pushed forward to see what was the matter, and cried out in astonishment:

"For goodness' sake!"

Then the three stood motionless, staring hard, until Polychrome's merry laughter rang out behind them and aroused them from their stupor.

In the path before them stood a tin man who was the exact duplicate of the Tin Woodman. He was of the same size, he was jointed in the same manner, and he was made of shining tin from top to toe. But he stood immovable, with his tin jaws half parted and his tin eyes turned upward. In one of his hands was held a long, gleaming sword. Yes, *there* was the difference, the only thing that distinguished him from the Emperor of the Winkies. This tin man bore a sword, while the Tin Woodman bore an axe.

"It's a dream; it *must* be a dream!" gasped Woot.

"That's it, of course," said the Scarecrow; "there couldn't be *two* Tin Woodmen."

"No," agreed Polychrome, dancing nearer to the stranger, "this one is a Tin Soldier. Don't you see his sword?"

The Tin Woodman cautiously put out one tin hand and felt of his double's arm. Then he said in a voice that trembled with emotion:

"Who are you, friend?"

There was no reply.

"Can't you see he's rusted, just as you were once?" asked Polychrome, laughing again. "Here, Nick Chopper, lend me your oil-can a minute!"

The Tin Woodman silently handed her his oil-can, without which he never traveled, and Polychrome first oiled the stranger's tin jaws and then worked them gently to and fro until the Tin Soldier said:

"That's enough. Thank you. I can now talk. But please oil my other joints."

Woot seized the oil-can and did this, but all the others helped wiggle the soldier's joints as soon as they were oiled, until they moved freely.

The Tin Soldier seemed highly pleased at his release. He strutted up and down the path, saying in a high, thin voice:

"The Soldier is a splendid man
    When marching on parade,
And when he meets the enemy
    He never is afraid.
He rights the wrongs of nations,
    His country's flag defends,
The foe he'll fight with great delight,
    But seldom fights his friends."

CHAPTER 16

"ARE you really a soldier?" asked Woot, when they had all watched this strange tin person parade up and down the path and proudly flourish his sword.

"I *was* a soldier," was the reply, "but I've been a prisoner to Mr. Rust so long that I don't know exactly *what* I am."

"But—dear me!" cried the Tin Woodman, sadly perplexed; "how came you to be made of tin?"

"That," answered the Soldier, "is a sad, sad story. I was in love with a beautiful Munchkin girl, who lived with a Wicked Witch. The

Witch did not wish me to marry the girl, so she enchanted my sword, which began hacking me to pieces. When I lost my legs I went to the tinsmith, Ku-Klip, and he made me some tin legs. When I lost my arms, Ku-Klip made me tin arms, and when I lost my head he made me this fine one out of tin. It was the same way with my body, and finally I was all tin. But I was not unhappy, for Ku-Klip made a good job of me, having had experience in making another tin man before me."

"Yes," observed the Tin Woodman, "it was Ku-Klip who made me. But, tell me, what was the name of the Munchkin girl you were in love with?"

"She is called Nimmie Amee," said the Tin Soldier.

Hearing this, they were all so astonished that they were silent for a time, regarding the stranger with wondering looks. Finally the Tin Woodman ventured to ask:

"And did Nimmie Amee return your love?"

"Not at first," admitted the Soldier. "When first I marched into the forest and met her, she was weeping over the loss of her former sweetheart, a woodman whose name was Nick Chopper."

"That is me," said the Tin Woodman.

"She told me he was nicer than a soldier, because he was all made of tin and shone beautifully in the sun. She said a tin man appealed to her artistic instincts more than an ordinary meat man, as I was then. But I did not despair, because her tin sweetheart had disappeared, and could not be found. And finally Nimmie Amee permitted me to call upon her and we became friends. It was then that the Wicked Witch discovered me and became furiously angry when I said I wanted to marry the girl. She enchanted my sword, as I said, and then my troubles began. When I got my tin legs, Nimmie Amee began to take an interest in me; when I got my tin arms, she began to like me better than ever, and when I was all made of tin, she said I looked like her dear Nick Chopper and she would be willing to marry me.

"The day of our wedding was set, and it turned out to be a rainy day. Nevertheless I started out to get Nimmie Amee, because the Witch had been absent for some time, and we meant to elope before she got back. As I traveled the forest paths the rain wetted my joints, but I paid no attention to this because my thoughts were all on my wedding with beautiful Nimmie Amee and I could think of nothing else until suddenly my legs stopped moving. Then my arms rusted at the joints and I became frightened and cried for help, for now I was unable to oil myself. No one heard my calls and before long my jaws rusted, and I was unable to utter another sound. So I stood helpless in this spot, hoping some wanderer would come my way and save me. But this forest path is seldom used, and I have been standing here so long that I have lost all track of time. In my mind I composed poetry and sang songs, but not a sound have I been able to utter. But this desperate condition has now been relieved by your coming my way and I must thank you for my rescue."

"This is wonderful!" said the Scarecrow, heaving a stuffy, long sigh. "I think Ku-Klip was wrong to make two tin men, just alike, and the strangest thing of all is that both you tin men fell in love with the same girl."

"As for that," returned the Soldier, seriously, "I must admit I lost my ability to love when I lost my meat heart. Ku-Klip gave me a tin heart, to be sure, but it doesn't love anything, as far as I can discover, and merely rattles against my tin ribs, which makes me wish I had no heart at all."

"Yet, in spite of this condition, you were going to marry Nimmie Amee?"

"Well, you see I had promised to marry her, and I am an honest man and always try to keep my promises. I didn't like to disappoint the poor girl, who had been disappointed by one tin man already."

"That was not my fault," declared the Emperor of the Winkies, and then he related how he, also, had rusted in the forest and after a long time had been rescued by Dorothy and the Scarecrow and had traveled with them to the Emerald City in search of a heart that could love.

"If you have found such a heart, sir," said the Soldier, "I will gladly allow you to marry Nimmie Amee in my place."

"If she loves you best, sir," answered the Woodman, "I shall not interfere with your wedding her. For, to be quite frank with you, I cannot yet love Nimmie Amee as I did before I became tin."

"Still, one of you ought to marry the poor girl," remarked Woot; "and, if she likes tin men, there is not much choice between you. Why don't you draw lots for her?"

"That wouldn't be right," said the Scarecrow.

"The girl should be permitted to choose her own husband," asserted Polychrome. "You should both go to her and allow her to take her choice. Then she will surely be happy."

"That, to me, seems a very fair arrangement," said the Tin Soldier.

"I agree to it," said the Tin Woodman, shaking the hand of his twin to show the matter was settled. "May I ask your name, sir?" he continued.

"Before I was so cut up," replied the other, "I was known as Captain Fyter, but afterward I was merely called 'The Tin Soldier.' "

"Well, Captain, if you are agreeable, let us now go to Nimmie Amee's house and let her choose between us."

"Very well; and if we meet the Witch, we will both fight her—you with your axe and I with my sword."

"The Witch is destroyed," announced the Scarecrow, and as they walked away he told the Tin Soldier of much that had happened in the Land of Oz since he had stood rusted in the forest.

"I must have stood there longer than I had imagined," he said thoughtfully.

The Workshop of Ku-Klip

CHAPTER 17

IT was not more than a two hours' journey to the house where Nimmie Amee had lived, but when our travelers arrived there they found the place deserted. The door was partly off its hinges, the roof had fallen in at the rear and the interior of the cottage was thick with dust. Not only was the place vacant, but it was evident that no one had lived there for a long time.

"I suppose," said the Scarecrow, as they all stood looking wonderingly at the ruined house, "that after the Wicked Witch was destroyed, Nimmie Amee became lonely and went somewhere else to live."

"One could scarcely expect a young girl to live all alone in a forest," added Woot. "She would want company, of course, and so I believe she has gone where other people live."

"And perhaps she is still crying her poor little heart out because no tin man comes to marry her," suggested Polychrome.

"Well, in that case, it is the clear duty of you two tin persons to seek Nimmie Amee until you find her," declared the Scarecrow.

"I do not know where to look for the girl," said the Tin Soldier, "for I am almost a stranger to this part of the country."

"I was born here," said the Tin Woodman, "but the forest has few inhabitants except the wild beasts. I cannot think of anyone living near here with whom Nimmie Amee might care to live."

"Why not go to Ku-Klip and ask him what has become of the girl?" proposed Polychrome.

That struck them all as being a good suggestion, so once more they started to tramp through the forest, taking the direct path to Ku-Klip's house, for both the tin twins knew the way, having followed it many times.

Ku-Klip lived at the far edge of the great forest, his house facing the broad plains of the Munchkin Country that lay to the eastward. But, when they came to this residence by the forest's edge, the tinsmith was not at home.

It was a pretty place, all painted dark blue with trimmings of lighter blue. There was a neat blue fence around the yard and several blue benches had been placed underneath the shady blue trees which marked the line between forest and plain. There was a blue lawn before the house, which was a good-sized building. Ku-Klip lived in the front part of the house and had his work-shop in the back part, where he had also built a lean-to addition, in order to give him more room.

Although they found the tinsmith absent on their arrival, there was smoke coming out of his chimney, which proved that he would soon return.

"And perhaps Nimmie Amee will be with him," said the Scarecrow in a cheerful voice.

While they waited, the Tin Woodman went to the door of the workshop and, finding it unlocked, entered and looked curiously around the room where he had been made.

"It seems almost like home to me," he told his friends, who had followed him in. "The first time I came here I had lost a leg, so I had to carry it in my hand while I hopped on the other leg all the way from the place in the forest where the enchanted axe cut me. I remember that old Ku-Klip carefully put my meat leg into a barrel—I think that is the same barrel, still standing in the corner yonder—and then at once he began to make a tin leg for me. He worked fast and with skill, and I was much interested in the job."

"My experience was much the same," said the Tin Soldier. "I used to bring all the parts of me, which the enchanted sword had cut away, here to the tinsmith, and Ku-Klip would put them into the barrel."

"I wonder," said Woot, "if those cast-off parts of you two unfortunates are still in that barrel in the corner?"

"I suppose so," replied the Tin Woodman. "In the Land of Oz no part of a living creature can ever be destroyed."

"If that is true, how was that Wicked Witch destroyed?" inquired Woot.

"Why, she was very old and was all dried up and withered before Oz became a fairyland," explained the Scarecrow. "Only her magic arts had kept her alive so long, and when Dorothy's house fell upon her she just turned to dust, and was blown away and scattered by the wind. I do not think, however, that the parts cut away from these two young men could ever be entirely destroyed and, if they are still in those barrels, they are likely to be just the same as when the enchanted axe or sword severed them."

"It doesn't matter, however," said the Tin Woodman; "our tin bodies are more brilliant and durable, and quite satisfy us."

"Yes, the tin bodies are best," agreed the Tin Soldier. "Nothing can hurt them."

"Unless they get dented or rusted," said Woot, but both the tin men frowned on him.

Scraps of tin, of all shapes and sizes, lay scattered around the workshop. Also there were hammers and anvils and soldering irons and a charcoal furnace and many other tools such as a tinsmith works with. Against two of the side walls had been built stout work-benches and in the center of the room was a long table. At the end of the shop, which adjoined the dwelling, were several cupboards.

After examining the interior of the workshop until his curiosity was satisfied, Woot said:

"I think I will go outside until Ku-Klip comes. It does not seem quite proper for us to take possession of his house while he is absent."

"That is true," agreed the Scarecrow, and they were all about to leave the room when the Tin Woodman said: "Wait a minute," and they halted in obedience to the command.

CHAPTER 18

THE Tin Woodman had just noticed the cupboards and was curious to know what they contained, so he went to one of them and opened the door. There were shelves inside, and upon one of the shelves which was about on a level with his tin chin the Emperor discovered a Head—it looked like a doll's head, only it was larger, and he soon saw it was the Head of some person. It was facing the Tin Woodman and as the cupboard door swung back, the eyes of the Head slowly opened and looked at him. The Tin Woodman was not at all surprised, for in the Land of Oz one runs into magic at every turn.

"Dear me!" said the Tin Woodman, staring hard. "It seems as if I had met you, somewhere, before. Good morning, sir!"

"You have the advantage of me," replied the Head. "I never saw you before in my life."

"Still, your face is very familiar," persisted the Tin Woodman. "Pardon me, but may I ask if you—eh—eh—if you ever had a Body?"

"Yes, at one time," answered the Head, "but that is so long ago I can't remember it. Did you think," with a pleasant smile, "that I was born just as I am? That a Head would be created without a Body?"

"No, of course not," said the other. "But how came you to lose your body?"

"Well, I can't recollect the details; you'll have to ask Ku-Klip about it," returned the Head. "For, curious as it may seem to you, my memory is not good since my separation from the rest of me. I still possess my brains and my intellect is as good as ever, but my memory of some of the events I formerly experienced is quite hazy."

"How long have you been in this cupboard?" asked the Emperor.

"I don't know."

"Haven't you a name?"

"Oh, yes," said the Head; "I used to be called Nick Chopper, when I was a woodman and cut down trees for a living."

"Good gracious!" cried the Tin Woodman in

astonishment. "If you are Nick Chopper's Head, then you are *Me*—or I'm *You*—or—or— What relation *are* we, anyhow?"

"Don't ask me," replied the Head. "For my part, I'm not anxious to claim relationship with any common, manufactured article, like you. You may be all right in your class, but your class isn't my class. You're tin."

The poor Emperor felt so bewildered that for a time he would only stare at his old Head in silence. Then he said:

"I must admit that I wasn't at all bad looking before I became tin. You're almost handsome—for meat. If your hair was combed, you'd be quite attractive."

"How do you expect me to comb my hair without help?" demanded the Head, indignantly. "I used to keep it smooth and neat, when I had arms, but after I was removed from the rest of me, my hair got mussed, and old Ku-Klip never has combed it for me."

"I'll speak to him about it," said the Tin Woodman. "Do you remember loving a pretty Munchkin girl named Nimmie Amee?"

"No," answered the Head. "That is a foolish question. The heart in my body—when I had a body—might have loved someone, for all I know, but a head isn't made to love; it's made to think."

"Oh; do you think, then?"

"I used to think."

"You must have been shut up in this cupboard for years and years. What have you thought about, in all that time?"

"Nothing. That's another foolish question. A little reflection will convince you that I have had nothing to think about, except the boards on the inside of the cupboard door, and it didn't take me long to think of everything about those boards that could be thought of. Then, of course, I quit thinking."

"And are you happy?"

"Happy? What's that?"

"Don't you know what happiness is?" inquired the Tin Woodman.

"I haven't the faintest idea whether it's round or square, or black or white, or what it is. And, if you will pardon my lack of interest in it, I will say that I don't care."

The Tin Woodman was much puzzled by these answers. His traveling companions had grouped themselves at his back, and had fixed their eyes on the Head and listened to the conversation with much interest, but until now, they had not interrupted because they thought the Tin Woodman had the best right to talk to his own head and renew acquaintance with it.

But now the Tin Soldier remarked:

"I wonder if *my* old head happens to be in any of these cupboards," and he proceeded to open all the cupboard doors. But no other head was to be found on any of the shelves.

"Oh, well; never mind," said Woot the Wanderer; "I can't imagine what anyone wants of a cast-off head, anyhow."

"I can understand the Soldier's interest," asserted Polychrome, dancing around the grimy workshop until her draperies formed a cloud around her dainty form. "For sentimental reasons a man might like to see his old head once more, just as one likes to revisit an old home."

"And then to kiss it good-bye," added the Scarecrow.

"I hope that tin thing won't try to kiss *me* good-bye!" exclaimed the Tin Woodman's former head. "And I don't see what right you folks have to disturb my peace and comfort, either."

"You belong to me," the Tin Woodman declared.

"I do not!"

"You and I are one."

"We've been parted," asserted the Head. "It would be unnatural for me to have any interest in a man made of tin. Please close the door and leave me alone."

"I did not think that my old Head could be so disagreeable," said the Emperor. "I—I'm quite ashamed of myself; meaning *you*."

"You ought to be glad that I've enough sense to know what my rights are," retorted the Head. "In this cupboard I am leading a simple life, peaceful and dignified, and when a mob of people in whom I am not interested disturb me, *they* are the disagreeable ones; not I."

With a sigh the Tin Woodman closed and latched the cupboard door and turned away.

"Well," said the Tin Soldier, "if my old head would have treated me as coldly and in so unfriendly a manner as your old head has treated you, friend Chopper, I'm glad I could not find it."

"Yes; I'm rather surprised at my head, myself," replied the Tin Woodman, thoughtfully. "I thought I had a more pleasant disposition when I was made of meat."

But just then old Ku-Klip the Tinsmith arrived, and he seemed surprised to find so many visitors. Ku-Klip was a stout man and a short man. He had his sleeves rolled above his elbows, showing muscular arms, and he wore a leathern apron that covered all the front of him, and was so long that Woot was surprised he didn't step on it and trip whenever he walked. And Ku-Klip had a gray beard that was almost as long as his apron, and his head was bald on top and his ears stuck out from his head like two fans. Over his eyes, which were bright and twinkling, he wore big spectacles. It was easy to see that the tinsmith was a kind-hearted man, as well as a merry and agreeable one.

"Oh-ho!" he cried in a joyous bass voice; "here

are both my tin men come to visit me, and they and their friends are welcome indeed. I'm very proud of you two characters, I assure you, for you are so perfect that you are proof that I'm a good workman. Sit down. Sit down, all of you —if you can find anything to sit on—and tell me why you are here."

So they found seats and told him all of their adventures that they thought he would like to know. Ku-Klip was glad to learn that Nick Chopper, the Tin Woodman, was now Emperor of the Winkies and a friend of Ozma of Oz, and the tinsmith was also interested in the Scarecrow and Polychrome.

He turned the straw man around, examining him curiously, and patted him on all sides, and then said:

"You are certainly wonderful, but I think you would be more durable and steady on your legs if you were made of tin. Would you like me to—"

"No, indeed!" interrupted the Scarecrow hastily; "I like myself better as I am."

But to Polychrome the tinsmith said:

"Nothing could improve *you*, my dear, for you are the most beautiful maiden I have ever seen. It is pure happiness just to look at you."

"That is praise, indeed, from so skillful a workman," returned the Rainbow's Daughter, laughing and dancing in and out of the room.

"Then it must be this boy you wish me to

help," said Ku-Klip, looking at Woot.

"No," said Woot, "we are not here to seek your skill, but have merely come to you for information."

Then, between them, they related their search for Nimmie Amee, whom the Tin Woodman explained he had resolved to marry, yet who had promised to become the bride of the Tin Soldier before he unfortunately became rusted. And when the story was told, they asked Ku-Klip if he knew what had become of Nimmie Amee.

"Not exactly," replied the old man, "but I know that she wept bitterly when the Tin Soldier did not come to marry her, as he had promised to do. The old Witch was so provoked at the girl's tears that she beat Nimmie Amee with her crooked stick and then hobbled away to gather some magic herbs, with which she intended to transform the girl into an old hag, so that no one would again love her or care to marry her. It was while she was away on this errand that Dorothy's house fell on the Wicked Witch, and she turned to dust and blew away. When I heard this good news, I sent Nimmie Amee to find the Silver Shoes which the Witch had worn, but Dorothy had taken them with her to the Emerald City."

"Yes, we know all about those Silver Shoes," said the Scarecrow.

"Well," continued Ku-Klip, "after that, Nim-

mie Amee decided to go away from the forest and live with some people she was acquainted with who had a house on Mount Munch. I have never seen the girl since."

"Do you know the name of the people on Mount Munch, with whom she went to live?" asked the Tin Woodman.

"No, Nimmie Amee did not mention her friend's name, and I did not ask her. She took with her all that she could carry of the goods that were in the Witch's house, and she told me I could have the rest. But when I went there I found nothing worth taking except some magic powders that I did not know how to use, and a bottle of Magic Glue."

"What is Magic Glue?" asked Woot.

"It is a magic preparation with which to mend people when they cut themselves. One time, long ago, I cut off one of my fingers by accident, and I carried it to the Witch, who took down her bottle and glued it on again for me. See!" showing them his finger, "it is as good as ever it was. No one else that I ever heard of had this Magic Glue, and of course when Nick Chopper cut himself to pieces with his enchanted axe and Captain Fyter cut himself to pieces with his enchanted sword, the Witch would not mend them, or allow me to glue them together, because she had herself wickedly enchanted the axe and sword. Nothing remained but for me to make them new parts out of tin; but, as you see, tin answered the purpose very well, and I am sure their tin bodies are a great improvement on their meat bodies."

"Very true," said the Tin Soldier.

"I quite agree with you," said the Tin Woodman. "I happened to find my old head in your cupboard, a while ago, and certainly it is not as desirable a head as the tin one I now wear."

"By the way," said the Tin Soldier, "what ever became of *my* old head, Ku-Klip?"

"And of the different parts of our bodies?" added the Tin Woodman.

"Let me think a minute," replied Ku-Klip. "If I remember right, you two boys used to bring me most of your parts, when they were cut off, and I saved them in that barrel in the corner. You must not have brought me all the parts, for when I made Chopfyt I had hard work finding enough pieces to complete the job. I finally had to finish him with one arm."

"Who is Chopfyt?" inquired Woot.

"Oh, haven't I told you about Chopfyt?" exclaimed Ku-Klip. "Of course not! And he's quite a curiosity, too. You'll be interested in hearing about Chopfyt. This is how he happened:

"One day, after the Witch had been destroyed and Nimmie Amee had gone to live with her friends on Mount Munch, I was looking around the shop for something and came upon the bottle of Magic Glue which I had brought from the old Witch's house. It occurred to me to piece together the odds and ends of you two people, which of course were just as good as ever, and see if I couldn't make a man out of them. If I succeeded, I would have an assistant to help me with my work, and I thought it would be a clever idea to put to some practical use the scraps of Nick Chopper and Captain Fyter. There were two perfectly good heads in my cupboard, and a lot of feet and legs and parts of bodies in the barrel, so I set to work to see what I could do.

"First, I pieced together a body, gluing it with the Witch's Magic Glue, which worked perfectly. That was the hardest part of my job, however, because the bodies didn't match up well and some parts were missing. But by using a piece of Captain Fyter here and a piece of Nick Chopper there, I finally got together a very decent body, with heart and all the trimmings complete."

"Whose heart did you use in making the body?" asked the Tin Woodman anxiously.

"I can't tell, for the parts had no tags on them and one heart looks much like another. After the body was completed, I glued two fine legs and feet onto it. One leg was Nick Chopper's and one was Captain Fyter's and, finding one leg longer than the other, I trimmed it down to make them match. I was much disappointed to

find that I had but one arm. There was an extra leg in the barrel, but I could find only one arm. Having glued this onto the body, I was ready for the head, and I had some difficulty in making up my mind which head to use. Finally I shut my eyes and reached out my hand toward the cupboard shelf, and the first head I touched I glued upon my new man."

"It was mine!" declared the Tin Soldier, gloomily.

"No, it was mine," asserted Ku-Klip, "for I had given you another in exchange for it—the beautiful tin head you now wear. When the glue had dried, my man was quite an interesting fellow. I named him Chopfyt, using a part of Nick Chopper's name and a part of Captain Fyter's name, because he was a mixture of both your cast-off parts. Chopfyt was interesting, as I said, but he did not prove a very agreeable companion. He complained bitterly because I had given him but one arm—as if it were my fault!—and he grumbled because the suit of blue Munchkin clothes, which I got for him from a neighbor, did not fit him perfectly."

"Ah, that was because he was wearing my old head," remarked the Tin Soldier. "I remember that head used to be very particular about its clothes."

"As an assistant," the old tinsmith continued, "Chopfyt was not a success. He was awkward with tools and was always hungry. He demanded something to eat six or eight times a day, so I wondered if I had fitted his insides properly. Indeed, Chopfyt ate so much that little food was left for myself; so, when he proposed, one day, to go out into the world and seek adventures, I was delighted to be rid of him. I even made him a tin arm to take the place of the missing one, and that pleased him very much, so that we parted good friends."

"What became of Chopfyt after that?" the Scarecrow inquired.

"I never heard. He started off toward the east, into the plains of the Munchkin Country, and that was the last I ever saw of him."

"It seems to me," said the Tin Woodman reflectively, "that you did wrong in making a man out of our cast-off parts. It is evident that Chopfyt could, with justice, claim relationship with both of us."

"Don't worry about that," advised Ku-Klip cheerfully; "it is not likely that you will ever meet the fellow. And, if you should meet him, he doesn't know who he is made of, for I never told him the secret of his manufacture. Indeed, you are the only ones who know of it, and you may keep the secret to yourselves, if you wish to."

"Never mind Chopfyt," said the Scarecrow. "Our business now is to find poor Nimmie Amee and let her choose her tin husband. To do that, it seems, from the information Ku-Klip has given us, we must travel to Mount Munch."

"If that's the programme, let us start at once," suggested Woot.

So they all went outside, where they found Polychrome dancing about among the trees and talking with the birds and laughing as merrily as if she had not lost her Rainbow and so been separated from all her fairy sisters.

They told her they were going to Mount Munch, and she replied:

"Very well; I am as likely to find my Rainbow there as here, and any other place is as likely as there. It all depends on the weather. Do you think it looks like rain?"

They shook their heads, and Polychrome laughed again and danced on after them when they resumed their journey.

The Invisible Country

CHAPTER 19

THEY were proceeding so easily and comfortably on their way to Mount Munch that Woot said in a serious tone of voice:

"I'm afraid something is going to happen."

"Why?" asked Polychrome, dancing around the group of travelers.

"Because," said the boy, thoughtfully, "I've noticed that when we have the least reason for getting into trouble, something is sure to go wrong. Just now the weather is delightful; the grass is beautifully blue and quite soft to our feet; the mountain we are seeking shows clearly in the distance and there is no reason anything should happen to delay us in getting there. Our troubles all seem to be over, and—well, that's why I'm afraid," he added, with a sigh.

"Dear me!" remarked the Scarecrow, "what unhappy thoughts you have, to be sure. This is proof that born brains cannot equal manufactured brains, for *my* brains dwell only on facts and never borrow trouble. When there is occasion for my brains to think, they think, but I would be ashamed of my brains if they kept shooting out thoughts that were merely fears and imaginings, such as do no good, but are likely to do harm."

"For my part," said the Tin Woodman, "I do not think at all, but allow my velvet heart to guide me at all times."

"The tinsmith filled my hollow head with scraps and clippings of tin," said the Soldier, "and he told me they would do nicely for brains, but when I begin to think, the tin scraps rattle around and get so mixed that I'm soon bewildered. So I try not to think. My tin heart is almost as useless to me, for it is hard and cold, so I'm sure the red velvet heart of my friend Nick Chopper is a better guide."

"Thoughtless people are not unusual," observed the Scarecrow, "but I consider them more fortunate than those who have useless or wicked thoughts and do not try to curb them. Your oil-can, friend Woodman, is filled with oil, but you only apply the oil to your joints, drop by drop, as you need it, and do not keep spilling it where it will do no good. Thoughts should be restrained in the same way as your oil, and only applied when necessary, and for a good purpose. If used carefully, thoughts are good things to have."

Polychrome laughed at him, for the Rainbow's Daughter knew more about thoughts than the Scarecrow did. But the others were solemn, feeling they had been rebuked, and tramped on in silence.

Suddenly Woot, who was in the lead, looked around and found that all his comrades had mysteriously disappeared. But where could they have gone to? The broad plain was all about him and there were neither trees nor bushes that could hide even a rabbit, nor any hole for one to fall into. Yet there he stood, alone.

Surprise had caused him to halt, and with a thoughtful and puzzled expression on his face he looked down at his feet. It startled him anew to discover that he had no feet. He reached out his hands, but he could not see them. He could feel his hands and arms and body; he stamped his feet on the grass and knew they were there, but in some strange way they had become invisible.

While Woot stood, wondering, a crash of metal sounded in his ears and he heard two heavy bodies tumble to the earth just beside him.

"Good gracious!" exclaimed the voice of the Tin Woodman.

"Mercy me!" cried the voice of the Tin Soldier.

"Why didn't you look where you were going?" asked the Tin Woodman reproachfully.

"I did, but I couldn't see you," said the Tin Soldier. "Something has happened to my tin eyes. I can't see you, even now, nor can I see anyone else!"

"It's the same way with me," admitted the Tin Woodman.

Woot couldn't see either of them, although he heard them plainly, and just then something smashed against him unexpectedly and knocked him over; but it was only the straw-stuffed body of the Scarecrow that fell upon him and while he could not see the Scarecrow he managed to push him off and rose to his feet just as Polychrome whirled against him and made him tumble again.

Sitting upon the ground, the boy asked:

"Can *you* see us, Poly?"

"No, indeed," answered the Rainbow's Daughter; "we've all become invisible."

"How did it happen, do you suppose?" inquired the Scarecrow, lying where he had fallen.

"We have met with no enemy," answered Polychrome, "so it must be that this part of the country has the magic quality of making people invisible—even fairies falling under the charm.

We can see the grass, and the flowers, and the stretch of plain before us, and we can still see Mount Munch in the distance; but we cannot see ourselves or one another."

"Well, what are we to do about it?" demanded Woot.

"I think this magic affects only a small part of the plain," replied Polychrome; "perhaps there is only a streak of the country where an enchantment makes people become invisible. So, if we get together and hold hands, we can travel toward Mount Munch until the enchanted streak is passed."

"All right," said Woot, jumping up, "give me your hand, Polychrome. Where are you?"

"Here," she answered. "Whistle, Woot, and keep whistling until I come to you."

So Woot whistled, and presently Polychrome found him and grasped his hand.

"Someone must help me up," said the Scarecrow, lying near them; so they found the straw man and sat him upon his feet, after which he held fast to Polychrome's other hand.

Nick Chopper and the Tin Soldier had managed to scramble up without assistance, but it was awkward for them and the Tin Woodman said:

"I don't seem to stand straight, somehow. But my joints all work, so I guess I can walk."

Guided by his voice, they reached his side,

where Woot grasped his tin fingers so they might keep together.

The Tin Soldier was standing near by and the Scarecrow soon touched him and took hold of his arm.

"I hope you're not wobbly," said the straw man, "for if two of us walk unsteadily we will be sure to fall."

"I'm not wobbly," the Tin Soldier assured him, "but I'm certain that one of my legs is shorter than the other. I can't see it, to tell what's gone wrong, but I'll limp on with the rest of you until we are out of this enchanted territory."

They now formed a line, holding hands, and turning their faces toward Mount Munch resumed their journey. They had not gone far, however, when a terrible growl saluted their ears. The sound seemed to come from a place just in front of them, so they halted abruptly and remained silent, listening with all their ears.

"I smell straw!" cried a hoarse, harsh voice, with more growls and snarls. "I smell straw and I'm a Hip-po-gy-raf who loves straw and eats all he can find. I want to eat *this* straw! Where is it? Where is it?"

The Scarecrow, hearing this, trembled but kept silent. All the others were silent, too, hoping that the invisible beast would be unable to find them. But the creature sniffed the odor of the straw and drew nearer and nearer to them until he reached the Tin Woodman, on one end of the line. It was a big beast and it smelled of the Tin Woodman and grated two rows of enormous teeth against the Emperor's tin body.

"Bah! that's not straw," said the harsh voice, and the beast advanced along the line to Woot.

"Meat! Pooh, you're no good! I can't eat meat," grumbled the beast, and passed on to Polychrome.

"Sweetmeats and perfume—cobwebs and dew! Nothing to eat in a fairy like you," said the creature.

Now, the Scarecrow was next to Polychrome in the line, and he realized if the beast devoured his straw he would be helpless for a long time, because the last farmhouse was far behind them and only grass covered the vast expanse of plain. So in his fright he let go of Polychrome's hand and put the hand of the Tin Soldier in that of the Rainbow's Daughter. Then he slipped back of the line and went to the other end, where he silently seized the Tin Woodman's hand.

Meantime, the beast had smelled the Tin Soldier and found he was the last of the line.

"That's funny!" growled the Hip-po-gy-raf; "I can smell straw, but I can't find it. Well, it's here, somewhere, and I must hunt around until I *do* find it, for I'm hungry."

His voice was now at the left of them, so they started on, hoping to avoid him, and traveled as fast as they could in the direction of Mount Munch.

"I don't like this invisible country," said Woot with a shudder. "We can't tell how many dreadful, invisible beasts are roaming around us, or what danger we'll come to next."

"Quit thinking about danger, please," said the Scarecrow, warningly.

"Why?" asked the boy.

"If you think of some dreadful thing, it's liable to happen, but if you don't think of it, and no one else thinks of it, it just *can't* happen. Do you see?"

"No," answered Woot. "I won't be able to see much of anything until we escape from this enchantment."

But they got out of the invisible strip of country as suddenly as they had entered it, and the instant they got out they stopped short, for just before them was a deep ditch, running at right angles as far as their eyes could see and stopping all further progress toward Mount Munch.

"It's not so very wide," said Woot, "but I'm sure none of us can jump across it."

Polychrome began to laugh, and the Scarecrow said: "What's the matter?"

"Look at the tin men!" she said, with another burst of merry laughter.

Woot and the Scarecrow looked, and the tin men looked at themselves.

"It was the collision," said the Tin Woodman regretfully. "I knew something was wrong with me, and now I can see that my side is dented in so that I lean over toward the left. It was the Soldier's fault; he shouldn't have been so careless."

"It is your fault that my right leg is bent, making it shorter than the other, so that I limp badly," retorted the Soldier. "You shouldn't have stood where I was walking."

"You shouldn't have walked where I was standing," replied the Tin Woodman.

It was almost a quarrel, so Polychrome said soothingly:

"Never mind, friends; as soon as we have time I am sure we can straighten the Soldier's leg and get the dent out of the Woodman's body. The Scarecrow needs patting into shape, too, for he had a bad tumble, but our first task is to get over this ditch."

"Yes, the ditch is the most important thing, just now," added Woot.

They were standing in a row, looking hard at the unexpected barrier, when a fierce growl from behind them made them all turn quickly. Out of the invisible country marched a huge beast with a thick, leathery skin and a surprisingly long neck. The head on the top of this neck was broad and flat and the eyes and mouth were very big and the nose and ears very small. When the

head was drawn down toward the beast's shoulders, the neck was all wrinkles, but the head could shoot up very high indeed, if the creature wished it to.

"Dear me!" exclaimed the Scarecrow, "this must be the Hip-po-gy-raf."

"Quite right," said the beast; "and you're the straw which I'm to eat for my dinner. Oh, how I love straw! I hope you don't resent my affectionate appetite?"

With its four great legs it advanced straight toward the Scarecrow, but the Tin Woodman and the Tin Soldier both sprang in front of their friend and flourished their weapons.

"Keep off!" said the Tin Woodman, warningly, "or I'll chop you with my axe."

"Keep off!" said the Tin Soldier, "or I'll cut you with my sword."

"Would you really do that?" asked the Hip-po-gy-raf, in a disappointed voice.

"We would," they both replied, and the Tin Woodman added: "The Scarecrow is our friend, and he would be useless without his straw stuffing. So, as we are comrades, faithful and true, we will defend our friend's stuffing against all enemies."

The Hip-po-gy-raf sat down and looked at them sorrowfully.

"When one has made up his mind to have a meal of delicious straw, and then finds he can't have it, it is certainly hard luck," he said. "And what good is the straw man to you, or to himself, when the ditch keeps you from going any further?"

"Well, we can go back again," suggested Woot.

"True," said the Hip-po; "and if you do, you'll be as disappointed as I am. That's some comfort, anyhow."

The travelers looked at the beast, and then they looked across the ditch at the level plain beyond. On the other side the grass had grown tall, and the sun had dried it, so there was a fine crop of hay that only needed to be cut and stacked.

"Why don't you cross over and eat hay?" the boy asked the beast.

"I'm not fond of hay," replied the Hip-po-gy-raf; "straw is much more delicious, to my notion, and it's more scarce in this neighborhood, too. Also I must confess that I can't get across the ditch, for my body is too heavy and clumsy for me to jump the distance. I can stretch my neck across, though, and you will notice that I've nibbled the hay on the farther edge—not because I liked it, but because one must eat, and if one can't get the sort of food he desires, he must take what is offered or go hungry."

"Ah, I see you are a philosopher," remarked the Scarecrow.

"No, I'm just a Hip-po-gy-raf," was the reply.

Polychrome was not afraid of the big beast. She danced close to him and said:

"If you can stretch your neck across the ditch, why not help us over? We can sit on your big head, one at a time, and then you can lift us across."

"Yes; I *can*, it is true," answered the Hip-po; "but I refuse to do it. Unless—" he added, and stopped short.

"Unless what?" asked Polychrome.

"Unless you first allow me to eat the straw with which the Scarecrow is stuffed."

"No," said the Rainbow's Daughter, "that is too high a price to pay. Our friend's straw is nice and fresh, for he was restuffed only a little while ago."

"I know," agreed the Hip-po-gy-raf. "That's why I want it. If it was old, musty straw, I wouldn't care for it."

"*Please* lift us across," pleaded Polychrome.

"No," replied the beast; "since you refuse my generous offer, I can be as stubborn as you are."

After that they were all silent for a time, but then the Scarecrow said bravely:

"Friends, let us agree to the beast's terms. Give him my straw, and carry the rest of me with you across the ditch. Once on the other side, the Tin Soldier can cut some of the hay with his sharp sword, and you can stuff me with that material until we reach a place where there is straw. It is true I have been stuffed with straw all my life and it will be somewhat humiliating to be filled with common hay, but I am willing to sacrifice my pride in a good cause. Moreover, to abandon our errand and so deprive the great Emperor of the Winkies—or this noble Soldier—of his bride, would be equally humiliating, if not more so."

"You're a very honest and clever man!" exclaimed the Hip-po-gy-raf, admiringly. "When I have eaten your head, perhaps I also will become clever."

"You're not to eat my head, you know," returned the Scarecrow hastily. "My head isn't stuffed with straw and I cannot part with it. When one loses his head he loses his brains."

"Very well, then; you may keep your head," said the beast.

The Scarecrow's companions thanked him warmly for his loyal sacrifice to their mutual good, and then he laid down and permitted them to pull the straw from his body. As fast as they did this, the Hip-po-gy-raf ate up the straw, and when all was consumed Polychrome made a neat bundle of the clothes and boots and gloves and hat and said she would carry them, while Woot tucked the Scarecrow's head under his arm and promised to guard its safety.

"Now, then," said the Tin Woodman, "keep your promise, Beast, and lift us over the ditch."

"M-m-m-mum, but that was a fine dinner!" said the Hip-po, smacking his thick lips in satisfaction, "and I'm as good as my word. Sit on my head, one at a time, and I'll land you safely on the other side."

He approached close to the edge of the ditch and squatted down. Polychrome climbed over his big body and sat herself lightly upon the flat head, holding the bundle of the Scarecrow's raiment in her hand. Slowly the elastic neck stretched out until it reached the far side of the ditch, when the beast lowered his head and permitted the beautiful fairy to leap to the ground.

Woot made the queer journey next, and then the Tin Soldier and the Tin Woodman went over, and all were well pleased to have overcome this serious barrier to their progress.

"Now, Soldier, cut the hay," said the Scarecrow's head, which was still held by Woot the Wanderer.

"I'd like to, but I can't stoop over, with my bent leg, without falling," replied Captain Fyter.

"What can we do about that leg, anyhow?" asked Woot, appealing to Polychrome.

She danced around in a circle several times without replying, and the boy feared she had not heard him; but the Rainbow's Daughter was merely thinking upon the problem, and presently she paused beside the Tin Soldier and said:

"I've been taught a little fairy magic, but I've

never before been asked to mend tin legs with it, so I'm not sure I can help you. It all depends on the good will of my unseen fairy guardians, so I'll try, and if I fail, you will be no worse off than you are now."

She danced around the circle again, and then laid both hands upon the twisted tin leg and sang in her sweet voice:

> "Fairy Powers, come to my aid!
> This bent leg of tin is made;
> Make it straight and strong and true,
> And I'll render thanks to you."

"Ah!" murmured Captain Fyter in a glad voice, as she withdrew her hands and danced away, and they saw he was standing straight as ever, because his leg was as shapely and strong as it had been before his accident.

The Tin Woodman had watched Polychrome with much interest, and he now said:

"Please take the dent out of my side, Poly, for I am more crippled than was the Soldier."

So the Rainbow's Daughter touched his side lightly and sang:

> "Here's a dent by accident;
> Such a thing was never meant.
> Fairy Powers, so wondrous great,
> Make our dear Tin Woodman straight!"

"Good!" cried the Emperor, again standing erect and strutting around to show his fine figure. "Your fairy magic may not be able to accomplish all things, sweet Polychrome, but it works splendidly on tin. Thank you very much."

"The hay—the hay!" pleaded the Scarecrow's head.

"Oh, yes; the hay," said Woot. "What are you waiting for, Captain Fyter?"

At once the Tin Soldier set to work cutting hay with his sword and in a few minutes there was quite enough with which to stuff the Scarecrow's body. Woot and Polychrome did this and it was no easy task because the hay packed together more than straw and as they had little experience in such work their job, when completed, left the Scarecrow's arms and legs rather bunchy. Also there was a hump on his back which made Woot laugh and say it reminded him of a camel, but it was the best they could do and when the head was fastened on to the body they asked the Scarecrow how he felt.

"A little heavy, and not quite natural," he cheerfully replied; "but I'll get along somehow until we reach a straw-stack. Don't laugh at me, please, because I'm a little ashamed of myself and I don't want to regret a good action."

They started at once in the direction of Mount Munch, and as the Scarecrow proved very clumsy in his movements, Woot took one of his arms and the Tin Woodman the other and so helped their friend to walk in a straight line.

And the Rainbow's Daughter, as before, danced ahead of them and behind them and all around them, and they never minded her odd ways, because to them she was like a ray of sunshine.

Over Night

CHAPTER 20

THE Land of the Munchkins
is full of surprises, as our
travelers had already learned,
and although Mount Munch
was constantly growing larger
as they advanced toward it,
they knew it was still a long
way off and were not certain,
by any means, that they had
escaped all danger or encountered their last adventure.

The plain was broad, and as far as the eye
could see, there seemed to be a level stretch of
country between them and the mountain, but
toward evening they came upon a hollow, in
which stood a tiny blue Munchkin dwelling

with a garden around it and fields of grain filling
in all the rest of the hollow.

They did not discover this place until they
came close to the edge of it, and they were astonished at the sight that greeted them because they
had imagined that this part of the plain had no
inhabitants.

"It's a very small house," Woot declared. "I
wonder who lives there?"

"The way to find out is to knock on the door
and ask," replied the Tin Woodman. "Perhaps
it is the home of Nimmie Amee."

"Is she a dwarf?" asked the boy.

"No, indeed; Nimmie Amee is a full-sized
woman."

"Then I'm sure she couldn't live in that little
house," said Woot.

"Let's go down," suggested the Scarecrow. "I'm
almost sure I can see a straw-stack in the back
yard."

They descended the hollow, which was rather
steep at the sides, and soon came to the house,
which was indeed rather small. Woot knocked
upon a door that was not much higher than his
waist, but got no reply. He knocked again, but
not a sound was heard.

"Smoke is coming out of the chimney," announced Polychrome, who was dancing lightly
through the garden, where cabbages and beets

and turnips and the like were growing finely.

"Then someone surely lives here," said Woot, and knocked again.

Now a window at the side of the house opened and a queer head appeared. It was white and hairy and had a long snout and little round eyes. The ears were hidden by a blue sunbonnet tied under the chin.

"Oh; it's a pig!" exclaimed Woot.

"Pardon me; I am Mrs. Squealina Swyne, wife of Professor Grunter Swyne, and this is our home," said the one in the window. "What do you want?"

"What sort of a Professor is your husband?" inquired the Tin Woodman curiously.

"He is Professor of Cabbage Culture and Corn Perfection. He is very famous in his own family, and would be the wonder of the world if he went abroad," said Mrs. Swyne in a voice that was half proud and half irritable. "I must also inform you intruders that the Professor is a dangerous individual, for he files his teeth every morning until they are sharp as needles. If you are butchers, you'd better run away and avoid trouble."

"We are not butchers," the Tin Woodman assured her.

"Then what are you doing with that axe? And why has the other tin man a sword?"

"They are the only weapons we have to defend

222

our friends from their enemies," explained the Emperor of the Winkies, and Woot added:

"Do not be afraid of us, Mrs. Swyne, for we are harmless travelers. The tin men and the Scarecrow never eat anything and Polychrome feasts only on dewdrops. As for me, I'm rather hungry, but there is plenty of food in your garden to satisfy me."

Professor Swyne now joined his wife at the window, looking rather scared in spite of the boy's assuring speech. He wore a blue Munchkin hat, with pointed crown and broad brim, and big spectacles covered his eyes. He peeked around from behind his wife and after looking hard at the strangers, he said:

"My wisdom assures me that you are merely travelers, as you say, and not butchers. Butchers have reason to be afraid of me, but you are safe. We cannot invite you in, for you are too big for our house, but the boy who eats is welcome to all the carrots and turnips he wants. Make yourselves at home in the garden and stay all night, if you like; but in the morning you must go away, for we are quiet people and do not care for company."

"May I have some of your straw?" asked the Scarecrow.

"Help yourself," replied Professor Swyne.

"For pigs, they're quite respectable," remarked Woot, as they all went toward the straw-stack.

"I'm glad they didn't invite us in," said Captain Fyter. "I hope I'm not too particular about my associates, but I draw the line at pigs."

The Scarecrow was glad to be rid of his hay, for during the long walk it had sagged down and made him fat and squatty and more bumpy than at first.

"I'm not specially proud," he said, "but I love a manly figure, such as only straw stuffing can create. I've not felt like myself since that hungry Hip-po ate my last straw."

Polychrome and Woot set to work removing the hay and then they selected the finest straw, crisp and golden, and with it stuffed the Scarecrow anew. He certainly looked better after the operation, and he was so pleased at being reformed that he tried to dance a little jig, and almost succeeded.

"I shall sleep under the straw-stack tonight," Woot decided, after he had eaten some of the vegetables from the garden, and in fact he slept very well, with the two tin men and the Scarecrow sitting silently beside him and Polychrome away somewhere in the moonlight dancing her fairy dances.

At daybreak the Tin Woodman and the Tin Soldier took occasion to polish their bodies and oil their joints, for both were exceedingly careful of their personal appearance. They had forgotten the quarrel due to their accidental bumping of one another in the invisible country, and being now good friends the Tin Woodman polished the Tin Soldier's back for him and then the Tin Soldier polished the Tin Woodman's back.

For breakfast the Wanderer ate crisp lettuce and radishes, and the Rainbow's Daughter, who had now returned to her friends, sipped the dewdrops that had formed on the petals of the wildflowers.

As they passed the little house to renew their journey, Woot called out:

"Good-bye, Mr. and Mrs. Swyne!"

The window opened and the two pigs looked out.

"A pleasant journey," said the Professor.

"Have you any children?" asked the Scarecrow, who was a great friend of children.

"We have nine," answered the Professor; "but they do not live with us, for when they were tiny piglets the Wizard of Oz came here and offered to care for them and to educate them. So we let him have our nine tiny piglets, for he's a good Wizard and can be relied upon to keep his promises."

"I know the Nine Tiny Piglets," said the Tin Woodman.

"So do I," said the Scarecrow. "They still live in the Emerald City, and the Wizard takes good care of them and teaches them to do all sorts of tricks."

"Did they ever grow up?" inquired Mrs. Squealina Swyne, in an anxious voice.

"No," answered the Scarecrow; "like all other children in the Land of Oz, they will always remain children, and in the case of the tiny piglets that is a good thing, because they would not be nearly so cute and cunning if they were bigger."

"But are they happy?" asked Mrs. Swyne.

"Everyone in the Emerald City is happy," said the Tin Woodman. "They can't help it."

Then the travelers said good-bye, and climbed the side of the basin that was toward Mount Munch.

Polychrome's Magic

CHAPTER 21

ON this morning, which ought to be the last of this important journey, our friends started away as bright and cheery as could be, and Woot whistled a merry tune so that Polychrome could dance to the music.

On reaching the top of the hill, the plain spread out before them in all its beauty of blue grasses and wildflowers, and Mount Munch seemed much nearer than it had the previous evening. They trudged on at a brisk pace, and by noon the mountain was so close that they could admire its appearance. Its slopes were partly clothed with pretty evergreens, and its foot-hills were tufted with a slender waving bluegrass that had a tassel on the end of every blade. And, for the first time, they perceived, near the foot of the mountain, a charming house, not of great size but neatly painted and with many flowers surrounding it and vines climbing over the doors and windows.

It was toward this solitary house that our travelers now directed their steps, thinking to inquire of the people who lived there where Nimmie Amee might be found.

There were no paths, but the way was quite open and clear, and they were drawing near to the dwelling when Woot the Wanderer, who was then in the lead of the little party, halted with such an abrupt jerk that he stumbled over backward and lay flat on his back in the meadow. The Scarecrow stopped to look at the boy.

"Why did you do that?" he asked in surprise.

Woot sat up and gazed around him in amazement.

"I—I don't know!" he replied.

The two tin men, arm in arm, started to pass them, when both halted and tumbled, with a great clatter, into a heap beside Woot. Polychrome, laughing at the absurd sight, came dancing up and she, also, came to a sudden stop, but managed to save herself from falling.

Everyone of them was much astonished, and the Scarecrow said with a puzzled look:

"I don't see anything."

"Nor I," said Woot; "but something hit me, just the same."

"Some invisible person struck me a heavy blow," declared the Tin Woodman, struggling to separate himself from the Tin Soldier, whose legs and arms were mixed with his own.

"I'm not sure it was a person," said Polychrome, looking more grave than usual. "It seems to me that I merely ran into some hard substance which barred my way. In order to make sure of this, let me try another place."

She ran back a way and then with much caution advanced in a different place, but when she reached a position on a line with the others she halted, her arms outstretched before her.

"I can feel something hard—something smooth as glass," she said, "but I'm sure it is not glass."

"Let me try," suggested Woot, getting up; but when he tried to go forward, he discovered the same barrier that Polychrome had encountered.

"No," he said, "it isn't glass. But what is it?"

"Air," replied a small voice beside him. "Solid air; that's all."

They all looked downward and found a sky-blue rabbit had stuck his head out of a burrow in the ground. The rabbit's eyes were a deeper blue than his fur, and the pretty creature seemed friendly and unafraid.

"Air!" exclaimed Woot, staring in astonishment into the rabbit's blue eyes; "whoever heard

of air so solid that one cannot push it aside?"

"You can't push *this* air aside," declared the rabbit, "for it was made hard by powerful sorcery, and it forms a wall that is intended to keep people from getting to that house yonder."

"Oh; it's a wall, is it?" said the Tin Woodman.

"Yes, it is really a wall," answered the rabbit, "and it is fully six feet thick."

"How high is it?" inquired Captain Fyter, the Tin Soldier.

"Oh, ever so high; perhaps a mile," said the rabbit.

"Couldn't we go around it?" asked Woot.

"Of course, for the wall is a circle," explained the rabbit. "In the center of the circle stands the house, so you may walk around the Wall of Solid Air, but you can't get to the house."

"Who put the air wall around the house?" was the Scarecrow's question.

"Nimmie Amee did that."

"Nimmie Amee!" they all exclaimed in surprise.

"Yes," answered the rabbit. "She used to live with an old Witch, who was suddenly destroyed, and when Nimmie Amee ran away from the Witch's house, she took with her just one magic formula—pure sorcery it was—which enabled her to build this air wall around her house—the house yonder. It was quite a clever idea, I think, for it doesn't mar the beauty of the landscape,

solid air being invisible, and yet it keeps all strangers away from the house."

"Does Nimmie Amee live there now?" asked the Tin Woodman anxiously.

"Yes, indeed," said the rabbit.

"And does she weep and wail from morning till night?" continued the Emperor.

"No; she seems quite happy," asserted the rabbit.

The Tin Woodman seemed quite disappointed to hear this report of his old sweetheart, but the Scarecrow reassured his friend, saying:

"Never mind, your Majesty; however happy Nimmie Amee is now, I'm sure she will be much happier as Empress of the Winkies."

"Perhaps," said Captain Fyter, somewhat stiffly, "she will be still more happy to become the bride of a Tin Soldier."

"She shall choose between us, as we have agreed," the Tin Woodman promised; "but how shall we get to the poor girl?"

Polychrome, although dancing lightly back and forth, had listened to every word of the conversation. Now she came forward and sat herself down just in front of the Blue Rabbit, her many-hued draperies giving her the appearance of some beautiful flower. The rabbit didn't back away an inch. Instead, he gazed at the Rainbow's Daughter admiringly.

"Does your burrow go underneath this Wall of Air?" asked Polychrome.

"To be sure," answered the Blue Rabbit; "I dug it that way so I could roam in these broad fields, by going out one way, or eat the cabbages in Nimmie Amee's garden by leaving my burrow at the other end. I don't think Nimmie Amee ought to mind the little I take from her garden, or the hole I've made under her magic wall. A rabbit may go and come as he pleases, but no one who is bigger than I am could get through my burrow."

"Will you allow us to pass through it, if we are able to?" inquired Polychrome.

"Yes, indeed," answered the Blue Rabbit. "I'm no especial friend of Nimmie Amee, for once she threw stones at me, just because I was nibbling some lettuce, and only yesterday she yelled

'Shoo!' at me, which made me nervous. You're welcome to use my burrow in any way you choose."

"But this is all nonsense!" declared Woot the Wanderer. "We are every one too big to crawl through a rabbit's burrow."

"We are too big *now*," agreed the Scarecrow, "but you must remember that Polychrome is a fairy, and fairies have many magic powers."

Woot's face brightened as he turned to the lovely Daughter of the Rainbow.

"Could you make us all as small as that rabbit?" he asked eagerly.

"I can try," answered Polychrome, with a smile.

And presently she did it—so easily that Woot was not the only one astonished. As the now tiny people grouped themselves before the rabbit's burrow the hole appeared to them like the entrance to a tunnel, which indeed it was.

"I'll go first," said wee Polychrome, who had made herself grow as small as the others, and into the tunnel she danced without hesitation. A tiny Scarecrow went next and then the two funny little tin men.

"Walk in; it's your turn," said the Blue Rabbit to Woot the Wanderer. "I'm coming after, to see how you get along. This will be a regular surprise party to Nimmie Amee."

So Woot entered the hole and felt his way

along its smooth sides in the dark until he finally saw the glimmer of daylight ahead and knew the journey was almost over. Had he remained his natural size, the distance could have been covered in a few steps, but to a thumb-high Woot it was quite a promenade. When he emerged from the burrow he found himself but a short distance from the house, in the center of the vegetable garden, where the leaves of rhubarb waving above his head seemed like trees. Outside the hole, and waiting for him, he found all his friends.

"So far, so good!" remarked the Scarecrow cheerfully.

"Yes; *so far*, but no farther," returned the Tin Woodman in a plaintive and disturbed tone of voice. "I am now close to Nimmie Amee, whom I have come ever so far to seek, but I cannot ask the girl to marry such a little man as I am now."

"I'm no bigger than a toy soldier!" said Captain Fyter, sorrowfully. "Unless Polychrome can make us big again, there is little use of our visiting Nimmie Amee at all, for I'm sure she wouldn't care for a husband she might carelessly step on and ruin."

Polychrome laughed merrily.

"If I make you big, you can't get out of here again," said she, "and if you remain little, Nimmie Amee will laugh at you. So make your choice."

"I think we'd better go back," said Woot seriously.

"No," said the Tin Woodman, stoutly, "I have decided that it's my duty to make Nimmie Amee happy, in case she wishes to marry me."

"So have I," announced Captain Fyter. "A good soldier never shrinks from doing his duty."

"As for that," said the Scarecrow, "tin doesn't shrink any to speak of, under any circumstances. But Woot and I intend to stick to our comrades, whatever they decide to do, so we will ask Polychrome to make us as big as we were before."

Polychrome agreed to this request and in half a minute all of them, including herself, had been enlarged again to their natural sizes. They then thanked the Blue Rabbit for his kind assistance, and at once approached the house of Nimmie Amee.

Nimmie Amee

CHAPTER 22

WE may be sure that at this moment our friends were all anxious to see the end of the adventure that had caused them so many trials and troubles. Perhaps the Tin Woodman's heart did not beat any faster, because it was made of red velvet and stuffed with sawdust, and the Tin Soldier's heart was made of tin and reposed in his tin bosom without a hint of emotion. However, there is little doubt that they both knew that a critical moment in their lives had arrived, and that Nimmie Amee's decision was destined to influence the future of one or the other.

As they assumed their natural sizes and the rhubarb leaves that had before towered above their heads now barely covered their feet, they looked around the garden and found that no person was visible save themselves. No sound of activity came from the house, either, but they walked to the front door, which had a little porch built before it, and there the two tinmen stood side by side while both knocked upon the door with their tin knuckles.

As no one seemed eager to answer the summons they knocked again; and then again. Finally they heard a stir from within and someone coughed.

"Who's there?" called a girl's voice.

"It's I!" cried the tin twins, together.

"How did you get there?" asked the voice.

They hesitated how to reply, so Woot answered for them:

"By means of magic."

"Oh," said the unseen girl. "Are you friends, or foes?"

"Friends!" they all exclaimed.

Then they heard footsteps approach the door, which slowly opened and revealed a very pretty Munchkin girl standing in the doorway.

"Nimmie Amee!" cried the tin twins.

"That's my name," replied the girl, looking at them in cold surprise. "But who can *you* be?"

"Don't you know me, Nimmie?" said the Tin

Woodman. "I'm your old sweetheart, Nick Chopper!"

"Don't you know *me*, my dear?" said the Tin Soldier. "I'm your old sweetheart, Captain Fyter!"

Nimmie Amee smiled at them both. Then she looked beyond them at the rest of the party and smiled again. However, she seemed more amused than pleased.

"Come in," she said, leading the way inside. "Even sweethearts are forgotten after a time, but you and your friends are welcome."

The room they now entered was cosy and comfortable, being neatly furnished and well swept and dusted. But they found someone there besides Nimmie Amee. A man dressed in the attractive Munchkin costume was lazily reclining in an easy chair, and he sat up and turned his eyes on the visitors with a cold and indifferent stare that was almost insolent. He did not even rise from his seat to greet the strangers, but after glaring at them he looked away with a scowl, as if they were of too little importance to interest him.

The tin men returned this man's stare with interest, but they did not look away from him because neither of them seemed able to take his eyes off this Munchkin, who was remarkable in having one tin arm—quite like their own tin arms.

"Seems to me," said Captain Fyter, in a voice that sounded harsh and indignant, "that you, sir, are a vile impostor!"

"Gently—gently!" cautioned the Scarecrow; "don't be rude to strangers, Captain."

"Rude?" shouted the Tin Soldier, now very much provoked; "why, he's a scoundrel—a thief! *The villain is wearing my own head!*"

"Yes," added the Tin Woodman, "and he's wearing my right arm! I can recognize it by the two warts on the little finger."

"Good gracious!" exclaimed Woot. "Then this must be the man whom old Ku-Klip patched together and named Chopfyt."

The man now turned toward them, still scowling.

"Yes, that is my name," he said in a voice like a growl, "and it is absurd for you tin creatures, or for anyone else, to claim my head, or arm, or any part of me, for they are my personal property."

"You? You're a Nobody!" shouted Captain Fyter.

"You're just a mix-up," declared the Emperor.

"Now, now, gentlemen," interrupted Nimmie Amee, "I must ask you to be more respectful to poor Chopfyt. For, being my guests, it is not polite for you to insult my husband."

"Your husband!" the tin twins exclaimed in dismay.

"Yes," said she. "I married Chopfyt a long

time ago, because my other two sweethearts had deserted me."

This reproof embarrassed both Nick Chopper and Captain Fyter. They looked down, shame-faced, for a moment, and then the Tin Wood-man explained in an earnest voice:

"I rusted."

"So did I," said the Tin Soldier.

"I could not know that, of course," asserted Nimmie Amee. "All I knew was that neither of you came to marry me, as you had promised to do. But men are not scarce in the Land of Oz. After I came here to live, I met Mr. Chopfyt, and he was the more interesting because he re-minded me strongly of both of you, as you were before you became tin. He even had a tin arm, and that reminded me of you the more."

"No wonder!" remarked the Scarecrow.

"But, listen, Nimmie Amee!" said the astonished Woot; "he really *is* both of them, for he is made of their cast-off parts."

"Oh, you're quite wrong," declared Polychrome, laughing, for she was greatly enjoying the confusion of the others. "The tin men are still themselves, as they will tell you, and so Chopfyt must be someone else."

They looked at her bewildered, for the facts in the case were too puzzling to be grasped at once.

"It is all the fault of old Ku-Klip," muttered the Tin Woodman. "He had no right to use our cast-off parts to make another man with."

"It seems he did it, however," said Nimmie Amee calmly, "and I married him because he resembled you both. I won't say he is a husband to be proud of, because he has a mixed nature and isn't always an agreeable companion. There are times when I have to chide him gently, both with my tongue and with my broomstick. But he is my husband, and I must make the best of him."

"If you don't like him," suggested the Tin Woodman, "Captain Fyter and I can chop him up with our axe and sword, and each take such parts of the fellow as belong to him. Then we are willing for you to select one of us as your husband."

Nimmie Amee

"That is a good idea," approved Captain Fyter, drawing his sword.

"No," said Nimmie Amee; "I think I'll keep the husband I now have. He is now trained to draw the water and carry in the wood and hoe the cabbages and weed the flower-beds and dust the furniture and perform many tasks of a like character. A new husband would have to be scolded —and gently chided—until he learns my ways. So I think it will be better to keep my Chopfyt, and I see no reason why you should object to him. You two gentlemen threw him away when you became tin, because you had no further use for him, so you cannot justly claim him now. I advise you to go back to your own homes and forget me, as I have forgotten you."

"Good advice!" laughed Polychrome, dancing.

"Are you happy?" asked the Tin Soldier.

"Of course I am," said Nimmie Amee; "I'm the mistress of all I survey—the queen of my little domain."

"Wouldn't you like to be the Empress of the Winkies?" asked the Tin Woodman.

"Mercy, no," she answered. "That would be a lot of bother. I don't care for society, or pomp, or posing. All I ask is to be left alone and not to be annoyed by visitors."

The Scarecrow nudged Woot the Wanderer.

"That sounds to me like a hint," he said.

"Looks as if we'd had our journey for nothing," remarked Woot, who was a little ashamed and disappointed because he had proposed the journey.

"I am glad, however," said the Tin Woodman, "that I have found Nimmie Amee, and discovered that she is already married and happy. It will relieve me of any further anxiety concerning her."

"For my part," said the Tin Soldier, "I am not sorry to be free. The only thing that really annoys me is finding my head upon Chopfyt's body."

"As for that, I'm pretty sure it is *my* body, or a part of it, anyway," remarked the Emperor of the Winkies. "But never mind, friend Soldier; let us be willing to donate our cast-off members to insure the happiness of Nimmie Amee, and be thankful it is not our fate to hoe cabbages and draw water—and be chided—in the place of this creature Chopfyt."

"Yes," agreed the Soldier, "we have much to be thankful for."

Polychrome, who had wandered outside, now poked her pretty head through an open window and exclaimed in a pleased voice:

"It's getting cloudy. Perhaps it is going to rain!"

Through the Tunnel

CHAPTER 23

IT didn't rain just then, although the clouds in the sky grew thicker and more threatening. Polychrome hoped for a thunder-storm, followed by her Rainbow, but the two tin men did not relish the idea of getting wet. They even preferred to remain in Nimmie Amee's house, although they felt they were not welcome there, rather than go out and face the coming storm. But the Scarecrow, who was a very thoughtful person, said to his friends:

"If we remain here until after the storm, and Polychrome goes away on her Rainbow, then we will be prisoners inside the Wall of Solid Air; so it seems best to start upon our return journey at once. If I get wet, my straw stuffing will be ruined, and if you two tin gentlemen get wet, you may perhaps rust again, and become useless. But even that is better than to stay here. Once we are free of the barrier, we have Woot the Wanderer to help us, and he can oil your joints and restuff my body, if it becomes necessary, for the boy is made of meat, which neither rusts nor gets soggy or moldy."

"Come along, then!" cried Polychrome from the window, and the others, realizing the wisdom of the Scarecrow's speech, took leave of Nimmie Amee, who was glad to be rid of them, and said good-bye to her husband, who merely scowled and made no answer, and then they hurried from the house.

"Your old parts are not very polite, I must say," remarked the Scarecrow, when they were in the garden.

"No," said Woot, "Chopfyt is a regular grouch. He might have wished us a pleasant journey, at the very least."

"I beg you not to hold us responsible for that creature's actions," pleaded the Tin Woodman. "We are through with Chopfyt and shall have nothing further to do with him."

Polychrome danced ahead of the party and led them straight to the burrow of the Blue Rabbit, which they might have had some difficulty in finding without her. There she lost no time in making them all small again. The Blue Rabbit was busy nibbling cabbage leaves in Nimmie Amee's garden, so they did not ask his permission but at once entered the burrow.

Even now the raindrops were beginning to fall, but it was quite dry inside the tunnel and by the time they had reached the other end, outside the circular Wall of Solid Air, the storm was at its height and the rain was coming down in torrents.

"Let us wait here," proposed Polychrome, peering out of the hole and then quickly retreating. "The Rainbow won't appear until after the storm and I can make you big again in a jiffy, before I join my sisters on our bow."

"That's a good plan," said the Scarecrow approvingly. "It will save me from getting soaked and soggy."

"It will save me from rusting," said the Tin Soldier.

"It will enable me to remain highly polished," said the Tin Woodman.

"Oh, as for that, I myself prefer not to get my pretty clothes wet," laughed the Rainbow's daughter. "But while we wait I will bid you all adieu. I must also thank you for saving me from that dreadful Giantess, Mrs. Yoop. You have been good and patient comrades and I have enjoyed our adventures together, but I am never so happy as when on my dear Rainbow."

"Will your father scold you for getting left on the earth?" asked Woot.

"I suppose so," said Polychrome gaily; "I'm always getting scolded for my mad pranks, as they are called. My sisters are so sweet and lovely and proper that they never dance off our Rainbow, and so they never have any adventures. Adventures to me are good fun, only I never like to stay too long on earth, because I really don't belong here. I shall tell my Father the Rainbow that I'll try not to be so careless again, and he will forgive me because in our sky mansions there is always joy and happiness."

They were indeed sorry to part with their dainty and beautiful companion and assured her of their devotion if they ever chanced to meet again. She shook hands with the Scarecrow and the Tin Men and kissed Woot the Wanderer lightly upon his forehead.

And then the rain suddenly ceased, and as the tiny people left the burrow of the Blue Rabbit, a glorious big Rainbow appeared in the sky and the end of its arch slowly descended and touched the ground just where they stood.

Woot was so busy watching a score of lovely maidens—sisters of Polychrome—who were leaning over the edge of the bow, and another score who danced gaily amid the radiance of the splendid hues, that he did not notice he was growing big again. But now Polychrome joined her sisters on the Rainbow and the huge arch lifted and slowly melted away as the sun burst from the clouds and sent its own white beams dancing over the meadows.

"Why, she's gone!" exclaimed the boy, and turned to see his companions still waving their hands in token of adieu to the vanished Polychrome.

The Curtain Falls

CHAPTER 24

WELL, the rest of the story is quickly told, for the return journey of our adventurers was without any important incident. The Scarecrow was so afraid of meeting the Hippo-gy-raf, and having his straw eaten again, that he urged his comrades to select another route to the Emerald City, and they willingly consented, so that the Invisible Country was wholly avoided.

Of course, when they reached the Emerald City their first duty was to visit Ozma's palace, where they were royally entertained. The Tin Soldier and Woot the Wanderer were welcomed as warmly as any strangers might be who had been the traveling companions of Ozma's dear old friends, the Scarecrow and the Tin Woodman.

At the banquet table that evening they related the manner in which they had discovered Nimmie Amee, and told how they had found her happily married to Chopfyt, whose relationship to Nick Chopper and Captain Fyter was so bewildering that they asked Ozma's advice what to do about it.

"You need not consider Chopfyt at all," replied the beautiful girl Ruler of Oz. "If Nimmie Amee is content with that misfit man for a husband, we have not even just cause to blame Ku-Klip for gluing him together."

"I think it was a very good idea," added little Dorothy, "for if Ku-Klip hadn't used up your cast-off parts, they would have been wasted. It's wicked to be wasteful, isn't it?"

"Well, anyhow," said Woot the Wanderer, "Chopfyt, being kept a prisoner by his wife, is too far away from anyone to bother either of you tin men in any way. If you hadn't gone where he is and discovered him, you would never have worried about him."

"What do you care, anyhow," Betsy Bobbin asked the Tin Woodman, "so long as Nimmie Amee is satisfied?"

"And just to think," remarked Tiny Trot, "that any girl would rather live with a mixture like Chopfyt, on far-away Mount Munch, than to be the Empress of the Winkies!"

"It is her own choice," said the Tin Woodman contentedly; "and, after all, I'm not sure the Winkies would care to have an Empress."

It puzzled Ozma, for a time, to decide what to do with the Tin Soldier. If he went with the Tin Woodman to the Emperor's castle, she felt that the two tin men might not be able to live together in harmony, and moreover the Emperor would not be so distinguished if he had a double constantly beside him. So she asked Captain Fyter if he was willing to serve her as a soldier, and he promptly declared that nothing would please him more. After he had been in her service for some time, Ozma sent him into the Gillikin Country, with instructions to keep order among the wild people who inhabit some parts of that unknown country of Oz.

As for Woot, being a Wanderer by profession, he was allowed to wander wherever he desired, and Ozma promised to keep watch over his future journeys and to protect the boy as well as she was able, in case he ever got into more trouble.

All this having been happily arranged, the Tin Woodman returned to his tin castle, and his chosen comrade, the Scarecrow, accompanied him on the way. The two friends were sure to pass many pleasant hours together in talking over their recent adventures, for as they neither ate nor slept they found their greatest amusement in conversation.